# MAKING UP FOR
# Lost Time

## Karin Kallmaker

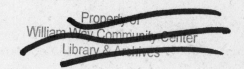
THE NAIAD PRESS, INC.
1998

Printed in the United States of America on acid-free paper
First Edition

Editor: Christine Cassidy
Cover designer: Bonnie Liss (Phoenix Graphics)
Typesetter: Sandi Stancil

Library of Congress Cataloging-in-Publication Data

Kallmaker, Karin, 1960 –
    Making up for lost time / by Karin Kallmaker.
        p.        cm.
    ISBN 1-56280-196-1   (pbk.)
    I. Title.
PS3561.A41665M34   1998
813'.54—dc21
                                                            97-51649
                                                                CIP

*For Maria, 21 years later*
*now if only it were legal*
*And Kelson, the man in my life*
*And HRH Eleanor*

*In memory of Betty Eilene Marja Ch'maj,*
*woman and scholar*

*The Eighth is for Eternity*

# Acknowledgments

My partner, Maria, who makes banana pancakes, pumpkin pie and cheese soufflé, as well as other goodies. The recipes for these treats are of her very own crafting; and

My mother, Florence, whose care in measuring and following directions set me a good example, which I too often ignore with disastrous culinary results; and

My grandmother, Marie, three-time baking sweepstakes champion of the Nevada County Fair, who taught me to knead bread and measure by a pinch of this, a dash of that and, when all else fails, add salt and hope for the best.

## About the Author

Karin Kallmaker was born in 1960 and raised by her loving, middle-class parents in California's Central Valley. The physician's Statement of Live Birth plainly declares, "Sex: Female" and "Cry: Lusty." Both are still true.

From a normal childhood and equally unremarkable public school adolescence, she went on to obtain an ordinary Bachelor's degree from the California State University at Sacramento. At the age of 16, eyes wide open, she fell into the arms of her first and only sweetheart. Ten years later, after seeing the film *Desert Hearts*, her sweetheart descended on the Berkeley Public Library determined to find some of "those" books. "Rule, Jane" led to "Lesbianism—Fiction" and then on to book after self-affirming book by and about lesbians. These books were the encouragement Karin needed to forget the so-called "mainstream" and spin her first romance for lesbians. That manuscript became her first Naiad Press book, *In Every Port*. She now lives in Oakland with that very same sweetheart; she is a one-woman woman. The happily-ever-after couple became mothers of Kelson in 1995 and Eleanor in 1997. They celebrate their twenty-first anniversary in 1998.

## Also by Karin Kallmaker

*Embrace in Motion*

*Wild Things*

*Painted Moon*

*Car Pool*

*Paperback Romance*

*Touchwood*

*In Every Port*

*Watermark* (forthcoming)

# Notes for the Unauthorized Biography

I was thirteen and waiting at the doctor's when I realized that my daddy owned one of the companies that printed several of the magazines on the table. *Sunrise, Tomorrow's Gourmet, Living Digest,* for example. It was the same story at the hair dresser, the dentist and the therapist. Wherever you wait my daddy has a good chance of grabbing some of your time.

When I was thirteen my father divorced his third

wife, my second stepmother. I told my therapist that it was okay that wives came and went in his life. He still loved my mother the most and if she were alive he'd still be married to her. I believed it then because my daddy told me so. He believed it then. He still believes it. It's convenient.

Maybe that's why I love him as much as I do for a man with an ego the size of a midwestern state and business scruples that would make the Mafia blush. He's strictly legal: he doesn't dump toxic waste or sell anything that causes cancer. He just makes money off the advertising by people who do.

They say that I'm a lot like him. The Paine Webber analysis on the parent company has a paragraph about me which includes the phrase "heir apparent." Nice of them not to say *heiress*. Heirs are presumed to work while heiresses spend. I do spend, that is true, but I work darned hard. Hard enough to be able to ask Daddy for business favors.

That was how it all began. I asked Daddy for a favor because a woman with blue-violet eyes had given me the perfect idea for mixing profitable business with extremely satisfying pleasure. I'd only met Valkyrie Valentine once. I'd never heard of Jamie Onassis — she's not related to *the* Onassis family. I have since come to the firm conclusion that women with big names are big trouble.

# German Chocolate Cookies

Make the Caramel Pecan Topping first

**Start with:**
1 cup each sugar
and evaporated milk
1/2 stick butter
1 tsp vanilla
3 egg yolks, beaten

Combine in a 2-quart saucepan, blending well. Stirring frequently, cook over medium heat for 10-13 minutes until mixture is thick and bubbly (it will look like caramel and be thick enough to coat a spoon). Remove from heat.

To the cooked mixture add:
1-3/4 cups flaked coconut and 1-1/4 cups chopped pecans

Allow mixture to cool to room temperature. Reserve 1-1/2 cups of it for topping the cookies; use the rest in the cookie dough (below). The topping is also tasty on ice cream!

Now make the cookie dough. Preheat oven to 350 degrees. You need:

1 package of "pudding in mix" style
German chocolate cake mix
1/3 cup butter, softened but not melted
All but 1.5 cups of the caramel topping you made above

Combine all of the ingredients in a large bowl. Stir gently until thoroughly moistened. Dough will be very soft.

Shape 1-inch balls with your hands (wash them first, of course!) and put on ungreased cookie sheets about 2 inches apart. Make a dent with your thumb in the center of each cookie. Don't worry if they split a little. Use a teaspoon to drop generous portions of the caramel topping you reserved into the dents. Bake for 11-14 minutes until flat and set. The "cracks" will look mostly dry. Err on the side of undercooking. Cool completely before trying to move the cookies.

Yields about 4 dozen unless a child helps; in this case you should monitor the inevitable quality-control sampling.

--Emily

# 1

Jamie ducked under a tray laden with large entree plates and snatched her pastry bag from the counter next to the rinse sink. "Damn it, Chuck, I wasn't done with it."

"Keep track of it then. Marcus told me to clean up."

*Fuck Marcus.* Jamie thought it as loudly as possible, aware that she could have said it and no one would have heard her over the din of the kitchen with all stations working at fever pace.

A waiter breezed by her, saying in passing, "I've got two chocolate soufflés, no raspberry on one."

"Two chocolate soufflés, no raspberry on one," Jamie echoed. She quickly whipped egg whites back to a stiff peak, then broke the frothy whites by slowly blending in a small amount of creamed dark chocolate. Then she poured the now cocoa-tinted whites back into the dark chocolate mixture, folding the two mixtures together with gentle strokes until dark and light were blended. She deftly filled two soufflé cups, neatly encircled with parchment chimneys, and set them in a baking pan quarter-full of hot water. She repeated to herself, "Steve's soufflés, timer number four," after she put the pan in the pastry oven.

She handled more than a dozen dessert orders before the soufflés were done. She enjoyed the artistic end a little bit, but filling in for the flu-stricken pastry chef for the night was intense. She flocked deep blue plates with powdered sugar, then ladled on nearly black chocolate sauce. Teaspoon dollops of white chocolate sauce followed around the perimeter of the dark sauce, then she used toothpicks as paintbrushes to create decorative whorls in the white sauce. She carefully set truffles with mint-chocolate leaves and other decorations on the beds of sauces just as she had seen Antoine do every night for the last four months. Marcus had not been happy when Antoine had insisted Jamie fill in for him.

She took a short mental break after what seemed like the umpteenth Chocolate Curl Fantasy — a scoop of lemon ice surrounded by long, sensuous curls of four different chocolates — and wondered what Aunt Emily would think of the desserts. They looked nothing like anything Aunt Em had ever served at her boardinghouse, but the boardinghouse guests had left the table just as pleased and a whole lot less poor. Jamie yummed to herself — a slab of bread and cinnamon-roll pudding with buttered rum sauce would be delicious right about now.

When the soufflés were done she arranged thick milk-chocolate curls on more powdered-sugar-flocked plates, then set the cups with their towers of soufflé in place in the center of each. The waiter arrived just as she finished and whisked them and a single bowl of chilled raspberries away while Jamie followed with a boat of warm milk-chocolate sauce. She liked Steve — he had a sense of panache. At tableside he punched down the soufflés like an artist, then stepped back with a flourish to let the chef-hatted, apron-wrapped Jamie add the final touch.

This part she loved. The guests were watching their soufflés deflate with equally deflated expressions, but when Jamie poured in the sauce and the soufflés swelled again their eyes lit up. Steve added the chilled raspberries to one plate while Jamie faded back to the kitchen.

At the end of the night, more then seventy-five desserts behind her, plus two dozen chocolate soufflés, Jamie heaved a sigh of relief when the bus crew came in to finish cleaning in the kitchen.

Juan and Taikem gave her heartfelt looks of gratitude upon discovering that she had already dumped her many bowls and saucepans into one of the sinks to soak. Antoine was not as tidy. But Jamie had learned to appreciate tidiness after years of scrubbing up after her aunt. Aunt Emily cooked fast and economically in terms of pans used, but she could never be described as neat.

Marcus suddenly loomed over her. "You were behind. Some of the waiters complained."

Jamie knew she had not been behind. She clenched her teeth and counted to ten.

Steve's voice floated over from the other side of the kitchen where the waiters were putting on their raincoats. "If you're talking about what I said earlier, it was somebody complaining that the soufflé took twenty-five minutes — typical tourist. The menu even says to allow thirty minutes and they complain when Jamie does it in twenty-five."

Jamie was grateful to Steve for putting in a good word, but she knew it was pointless. Marcus disliked her as intensely as he disliked all women. He barely tolerated them as waiters but certainly did not want one in his kitchen. He probably believed that Jamie's ovaries would somehow spoil the soup.

The waiters were disappearing into the rainy night. With the aroma of food dissipating, Jamie could smell wet sidewalk and damp asphalt. Between the rows of workstations and hanging pots and pans, Jamie saw Steve glance in her direction. She shook her head slightly — she was not in need of any white-charger routine on his part. It was only delaying the inevitable.

"I don't know why Antoine puts up with your standards," Marcus said sharply. "The desserts were sloppy. I'm sure everyone noticed. Word will get out and that's it — we're out of business. Do you have any idea the perfection it takes to keep a five-star restaurant in business? Do you think people pay eleven dollars plus tax and tip for a messy soufflé?"

He paused as if waiting for an answer. She knew he just wanted her to open her mouth as if to answer

8

so he could cut her off. She didn't give him the satisfaction, which just made him more angry. His face was so red she wondered if he'd have an apoplectic fit on the spot. No such luck, she thought, then mentally smacked herself for an impulse Aunt Emily would have considered uncharitable.

He began his favorite rant. "I've sunk everything I own into this place, and people like you are going to run me into the ground . . ."

Not strictly true, Jamie thought. Antoine owned half of the Fisherman's Wharf restaurant and had confided that last year he'd made more than ever before because of San Francisco tourism going up and the economy remaining strong. Enough people could afford eleven-dollar desserts.

She liked Antoine a lot — he was not easygoing by any means, but he wasn't a shrieker like Marcus, who ranted three or four times a night that they would close down. She stayed because she was still learning from both Marcus and Antoine. Antoine made breads and pastries with style and flavor — no guest ever left Le Monde feeling as if they'd eaten beautiful but flavorless air for dessert. And every week Marcus surprised her with a new entree — this week it had been roasted pork seared in mustard and brown sugar with a sweet Champagne, prune and apricot sauce. It was delicious. Jamie had sent the recipe to Aunt Em, noting that the addition of sweet potatoes and carrots would make the dish a hearty stew. The Champagne was optional.

Marcus was winding down and Jamie hadn't heard even half of it. If Antoine had been here he'd have shut Marcus off in midstream with one of his quiet observations.

"I really think we have to reevaluate your program here. You think you can just do the fun stuff. Antoine's spoiled you, letting a first-year intern handle pastries. You don't know a ganache from a giblet. When I left the C.I.A. I was happy to be a pantry chef for two years. Two years I chopped vegetables and made salads — not even dressings! Two years. And you're not even from a proper cooking academy. I don't know what he sees in you. I'd think you were sleeping together if he wasn't queer —"

"— just like you." Jamie hated it when Marcus called other people queer as if he wasn't himself. "Antoine will be back tomorrow and the pastries will be fine and I'll go back to salads and breads and you won't go out of business, okay?"

"Don't patronize me." Marcus bit off whatever he had been going to call her. Probably "you little bitch," which was his favorite phrase for everybody, male and female alike. He yanked his chef's hat off his head. "You think this is easy, you wear it." He twisted it and threw it on the floor, then stormed into the main restaurant to swear at the clean-up crew still wiping down chairs and vacuuming under tables.

Jamie's fingers only shook slightly as she folded her own chef's hat and then unwound her aprons. It had been a neat night — nothing had seeped through all three layers. She could head home without looking as if she'd bathed in her dinner. She'd seen Antoine finish the night looking as if he'd committed an ax murder.

Juan looked up from the sink. "I don't know how you take it."

"I don't listen," Jamie said. "It's how I deal with most men, except for you, darling Juan."

"And they say dykes don't flirt."

"Juan, I learned it all from you." It wasn't idle flattery. Juan had told Jamie she was too serious, so she had tried to pick up some of his glib ways with marginal results. As for being a dyke — well, she hoped there was no minimum requirement for number of lovers to qualify for dykehood. Judging from the personals and articles in the local gay weeklies, her body count of one might not be enough to qualify.

When she stepped out into the dank night she lifted her face to the mist and inhaled the heavy scent of salty rain and drifting fog from the nearby bay. For a brief moment she was home in Mendocino again. She'd forgotten her coat and umbrella that morning, but the temperature couldn't have been below sixty. After two winters in Philadelphia this weather seemed tropical by comparison. Philadelphia was too cold in the winter and too hot in the summer, but the Culinary Science Academy had a good reputation without costing more than a graduate degree from Harvard. Marcus was always pointing out his own Culinary Institute of America credentials, but Jamie knew it had taken him twelve years to pay off the student loan.

Her extension classes were the "improper" academy credentials he scorned. When she'd learned all she could — to the point of feeling she would forget what she'd learned from Aunt Em — she'd decided enough was enough. No more classes and no more snow. She had nursed her ailing Hyundai back across the country, pausing briefly at the Continental Divide to heave her snowboots into a rest area trash can. San Francisco had been near enough to home and offered a wide range of opportunities. She'd settled in, found the job at Le Monde and worked her brains out, six days a week. Aunt Em's hours had been longer, seven days a week during the summer, but she'd been working for herself. Slaving for Marcus and Antoine was wearing thin.

The rain was washing away the stress of the day. She made her way from the crowded sidewalks of Fisherman's Wharf to the Columbus Street bus and from there to the Ocean Beach trolley to within a block of the three-bedroom apartment she shared with two other women. It was close quarters, but they all worked long, non-overlapping hours and saw each other very little. Chris was a flight attendant and was rarely home. Suzy would just be getting up for her shift at UC Med Center and would not be bothered by Jamie's shower to get the stench of the restaurant out of her hair. Who would have thought that so much good food could smell so foul put all together?

By the time Jamie got home she was soaked through and she decided hot chocolate and toast was recommended. KatzinJam yowled an urgent request when she opened the door. She said a weary hello to Suzy, quickly sprinkled some dry food in KatzinJam's empty bowl, then wriggled out of her wet, smelly clothes. Her shower was brief and very hot. When she emerged KatzinJam was disappearing into the closet where his favorite middle-of-the-night sleeping place could be found. Jamie knew that as soon as KatzinJam smelled the toast he'd be back.

Suzy was just rinsing out her late night breakfast dishes when Jamie padded into the kitchen to make hot chocolate.

"Want some?"

"I'd love it, but I'm running a bit late." Typical

Suzy. "This came for you, by the way. It was under the door when I got home."

"Thanks." Jamie glanced at the FedEx envelope. Probably from Aunt Em, who was fond of sending notes and recipes via overnight mail so that Jamie could still smell whatever she'd been making that day in Mendocino, four hours or so up the coast. She got out the milk and cocoa powder and was happy to find her whisk and saucepan where she'd left them. She and Suzy were very orderly, but Chris was a whirlwind.

"See ya," Suzy called from the front door.

"Later," Jamie answered, and then it was just her and KatzinJam in the apartment.

She slathered her favorite cranberry marmalade on the toast and settled into the apartment's one comfortable chair with the steaming mug, plate with toast and the FedEx within reach. With a sigh of pure pleasure, she put her feet up on the ottoman. Like most restaurant workers, relaxing to Jamie meant getting off her feet.

After a sustaining swallow of creamy hot chocolate, she opened Aunt Em's FedEx letter.

It smelled of vanilla. Sure enough, a seed fell out of the envelope along with several sheets of paper covered in her aunt's neatly penciled handwriting, a manila envelope and a picture. The picture was a studio portrait of Aunt Emily — snazzy. She'd written "A few months ago" on the back.

"Dearest Jamie," the letter began, "if you are reading this I am dead."

Jamie blinked several times, then shook her head. She had misread it, that was all.

"Dearest Jamie," she read again, "if you are

reading this I am dead." She clutched the arm of the chair, suddenly feeling she was falling. Her heart pounded as she struggled to comprehend the rest. "I learned not long ago that I was dying, and decided not to tell anyone, not even Kathy, until I absolutely had to. As I write I have only a few days left and forgive me if I ramble. My thoughts now are of you, and all you have meant to me. Kathy has been away on a trip and returns tomorrow and she will know when she sees me that I am going."

The next sentence was hard to follow; it had been erased several times.

"I figured that at this last point in my life I was allowed some privacy and the right to take care of my affairs my own way. So I went to a lawyer a month or more ago and have taken care of all the details. By now Jacob O'Rhuan will have disposed of my ashes off the coast, everything taken care of as I wanted. Liesel will see to that. I couldn't bear the idea of you or Liesel weeping next to my grave. Whenever you see the ocean you'll know I'm near. My legacy is the people I've loved and fed in my life, and that's quite a lot, as you know."

Jamie put the letter down and closed her eyes. For several minutes she could only breathe raggedly.

She would have told anyone who asked that Aunt Emily was the glue of her life — more than a mother, more than a teacher, more than a friend. But she couldn't have conveyed, not fully understanding it herself, the way Emily Smitt had been a part of her.

Her mind spun with unanswered questions. What had she died of? Had she suffered? When did it happen? Why had she kept Jamie away? Liesel — poor Liesel. Having to do this by herself. They had so many friends, and Liesel was a strong woman, but she must have felt so alone. It was the middle of the night — no sense calling her when she might be getting some badly needed sleep.

Other, murkier conflicts surfaced. How was Kathy — Aunt Emily's only child — handling this? Thinking of Kathy brought the usual twist of pain, tempered with compassion. Surely Kathy had seen past her problems with her mother during the final days. Perhaps she had even realized that her mother and Liesel hadn't deserved being called perverts — but that didn't bear thinking about. Hoping Kathy would change had cost Jamie too many years already. And yet she still ached for Kathy to realize that what Jamie could offer was as lasting and as true as the love between Aunt Emily and Liesel, between any two people, for that matter.

She hadn't had to confront death like this before. She hardly knew what she thought of an afterlife or if Aunt Em could watch over her. Maybe Aunt Em now knew, from some distant, happy place, that Jamie had become who she was — chef, hiker, sailor, lesbian — because Aunt Em had been those things, and Jamie had always longed to be just like her. And she'd succeeded reasonably well, except for when Kathy had refused to be Jamie's Liesel.

Jamie pressed her hands to her eyes. Stop thinking about that, she told herself sternly. You've got to cope with today, and that's enough.

When she was able, she finished her aunt's final letter. "I know you will forgive me for being so businesslike about my end. I'm sure it won't really surprise you. Of course I wish I'd known five years ago this was all the time I had for retirement. I'd have never sold the Waterview and could have left it to you. I know how you loved it. But getting some warning let me put my affairs in order. Liesel gets the house, of course, as the survivor on the deed. She has a very good pension from the Army so I know she's taken care of. I've saved a bit over the years and got a nice sum for the inn, and when you put everything together they make a tidy amount. I was rather surprised. I'm sure Kathy knew it down to the penny, but since she didn't approve of her mother's life I've decided not to give her the chance to disapprove of my money."

So Kathy hadn't reconciled with her. Kathy was still — Kathy.

"I want you to have it. I've always loved you as if you were my daughter, and you gave me such joy and love when you came into my life. Liesel loves you, too. Kathy's marrying a rich lawyer, and she just doesn't need this. You do. I want you to buy a place where you can cook the way you want to. Make yourself happy. Above all, beloved Jamie, make yourself happy. — Aunt Emily."

Aunt Emily was dead.

Kathy was getting married. To a man.

An hour passed before Jamie could make herself open the manila envelope.

She gasped, then went back to crying.


She was stiff and cramped when she awoke in the chair. KatzinJam was biting her ankle. Her head and eyes throbbed, and her back refused to straighten completely as she hobbled to the kitchen. KatzinJam bit her two more times before Jamie managed to pour some dry food into his bowl.

In a daze, she made herself a bowl of cereal and dumped a can of Katz's favorite food into his bowl, once again empty. After she rinsed up she found herself mechanically setting out ingredients. She was opening the can of evaporated milk before she fully realized what she was doing. German chocolate cookies were her favorite, and they never failed to provide comfort.

She halved the recipe in deference to the apartment's tiny oven and even tinier cookie sheets. Even with four cookie sheets in rotation, it took over an hour to turn out two dozen cookies. She settled in the comfy chair again with several warm cookies and a large glass of milk, while KatzinJam angled for complete possession of the ottoman.

The aroma and taste of the cookies took her back to the Waterview like no photograph ever could. They were probably her earliest memory of Aunt Em. She'd been so unhappy and frightened, abandoned to the care of a woman her mother had said was related to the half-sister of the man she thought might be Jamie's father. In other words, a perfect stranger who hadn't said no when Jamie's mother had asked if she could leave Jamie there while she "pulled herself together." Seven-year-old Jamie had been used to her mother's habit of parking her with people, but it was usually someone she knew. She'd learned to call a lot of people "Aunt" and "Uncle."

Somehow, she'd known her mother wouldn't be back that time. She'd heard the desperation in her mother's voice, and internalized, if not actually understood, her mother's last words to her: "I hear

17

the schools are good and the other kids seem real nice. Be good."

She curled into the corner of the chair, chewing on caramel and coconut. Her nose dripped steadily — the sleeve of her robe was a mess, but she didn't care.

Her gaze fell on the manila envelope and she felt dizzy. Her aunt had wanted Jamie to buy a place where she could cook the way she wanted. She could quit Le Monde today and start looking, but that required initiative. It required making a plan. Not today. Maybe tomorrow.

She couldn't make any plans until she had answers to some of her questions. To her relief, Antoine answered the phone when she called the restaurant and he easily agreed to give Jamie a few days off as bereavement leave. Marcus would have a fit.

She packed a small bag and left a note for Suzy. It was clear and breezy when she finally got into the Hyundai. KatzinJam scrambled into his accustomed place on the passenger seat. Highway 1 took longer, but she could stop to picnic at Seal Beach, just as she and Aunt Emily — and Liesel, when she'd been along — always had. She might as well start her journey with pleasant memories.

# Chicken Marsala

1 cup flour
1 tsp salt
1 tsp dried basil
4 skinless, boneless chicken breast halves
1/4 cup extra virgin olive oil
2 cloves garlic, chopped
2 Tbsp butter
9 oz. small button mushrooms
1/2 cup sweet Marsala wine or other
    drinking quality sweet sherry

Preheat oven to 350˚. Coat a 9x13 baking
dish with cooking spray or vegetable oil.
In a sturdy bag, combine flour, salt and
basil. Fold tightly and shake to mix. Cut
the chicken breasts into quarters.
Working 4 pieces at a time, put the
chicken pieces in the bag and shake until
well coated.
Warm the olive oil in a large frying pan
over medium-high heat. Add garlic and
chicken. Sauté about 8 minutes until
chicken is golden. Do not let oil smoke.
Move the chicken and garlic to the baking
dish and return the pan to heat. Deglaze
pan with the wine, then pour liquid over
chicken. Cover dish and bake about 20
minutes. Thoroughly cooked chicken is
opaque throughout. Serve over pilaf or
plain rice.

# Beef with Leeks and Fennel

1 Tbsp good quality olive oil
1/2 cup Burgundy or other dry red wine
1 lb. washed and finely sliced leeks
1 cup chick

*first pressing of oil: strongest flavored*

*region in Italy*

*Paper or plastic?*

*glaze?*

*plus some for the cook*

# 2

"You must think you're pretty good."

"No, just pretty capable." Valentine Valkyrie kept herself, always too eager to smile, as serious as possible. Her nose tickled. She hoped she didn't sound nasal.

"So tell me more about your concept." The agent looked bored to Val, as if he'd already made up his mind that whatever she had to say wasn't interesting, especially since she wasn't wearing anything low cut.

You're not boring, she told herself. She let herself smile, finally, and launched into her spiel.

"My concept is a one-hour program called *A Month of Sundays*. Instead of finding *This Old House* sorts of projects to fix up, we'll concentrate on more ordinary houses and apartments, suburban and urban, and show what can be done if the viewer is willing to invest four Sundays — four shows and four weeks per project. Everything from home renovation, interior design, adding a room for a nursery — there's a baby boom on you know — and the sort of undertaking that a typical homeowner will see as achievable." Don't babble, she reminded herself, even if his eyes were rolling back in his head. "The kind of project that can be done without a lathe, router or any of the other expensive equipment you'd find in *The Yankee Workshop*."

"Sort of like a women's show. Like what's her name, Lynette somebody."

Val gritted her teeth but kept her smile. "Somewhat like Lynette Jennings, yes, but Lynette stays almost exclusively inside the home and her projects are not covered in minute detail. We'll do the occasional outdoor project, some gardening, and like I said, devote four hours over four weeks to a single home, not five minutes. And I want to emphasize that the projects can be done by working people. You won't have to be unemployed to find the time to do my projects."

"You're aiming for cable?"

"Cable or PBS, yes."

"Hmm."

God, Val hated the "Hmm" moment. Her nose itched. All plastic surgeons should be shot.

"Well, it's an interesting idea." He looked bored

almost to sleep. "If I hear of any outfit looking for something like it I'll get back to you, Ms. Val . . . ky . . . Val."

Val shook the agent's limp hand and kept herself from wiping her hand on her slacks until she was out the door.

He'd get back to her, would he? Right. Not an ounce of interest in taking the project to Viacom Corporate for The Learning Channel. Or even to any of the local PBS stations.

She munched on an oversized cranberry-apple muffin from the bakery next to the Muni station and then shoved her way onto the N-Judah toward home. Her column was due at the end of the day and she needed to do one last proof.

The streetcar clanked through tunnels and up some of San Francisco's less challenging hills. All the while Val resisted the urge to rub her nose. It would just make it puffy. She opened her satchel then closed it again. Mr. Bored hadn't wanted even to look at her collection of clippings from her column in *Sunrise*. Given his lack of interest in anything she said, why on earth had he agreed to meet with her after she'd cornered him at the Bay Area Cable Producers convention?

She caught a glimpse of her reflection in the dirty window. Oh yeah. Sometimes she forgot. With her nose now suited to her face, men were certainly more eager to meet with her. Like Bored, however, they readily agreed to meetings but listened hardly at all once Val insisted they meet in an office, not a hotel bar.

*Maybe I should have kept the schnoz.* She looked at her profile. No, she was better off without the

Durante. Although unprepared for the dramatic change in her appearance without it, she was ready and more than capable of going in front of a camera, in addition to pounding a keyboard.

She popped open a diet Coke when she got home and changed out of her "I'm serious, damn it" suit into jeans and a sweatshirt. A favorite sweatshirt, too. Deep purple with white lettering: *That's Ms. Muffdiver to You*.

She tripped over the laundry pile on her way from the bedroom to the living room, dropped into her chair at the crowded desk and snapped on the lamp. The light wavered, then steadied. She remembered she hadn't picked up more fuses on her way by the hardware store and hoped that nothing blew just because she chose to turn on two lights and the computer. The precarious quality of the electrical supply was just one of the reasons the apartment rented at a minimum, which was still most of her budget. But she didn't have to have a roommate — pesky things.

She had just opened her document when the phone rang. Kim, her editor.

"I need it before five, please, Val. It'll keep me from killing myself."

"I'm just about done."

"Your food thing is really working, too. We've added three new food advertisers."

"Thanks. I try." No need to tell Kim just how much of her columns were imagination when it came to cooking. She had added some serving and menu ideas at Kim's behest, but it required some serious research. Food that didn't come out of a box first was a mystery to her. One ex-girlfriend had complained that Val could ruin Cheerios.

She now had a stack of useful cooking references — *Joy of Cooking* for one. It helped, to a point. She'd read the entry on folding egg whites six times and still didn't know what it meant, but she could use the word *fold* properly in a cooking sentence now.

"Could you mention some brand names? Pick anything. We might be able to corner some more advertisers that way."

"By brand?" She hated the idea.

"By brand, sweetie darling. And send it to me a.s.a.p. I've just got to have it this afternoon or heads will roll."

"That explains why all the men have high voices."

Kim snarked — an indelicate snort of laughter that Val enjoyed getting out of her from time to time. Kim was far too ladylike. "You are so bad."

"And you are too stressed."

"It's my job, sweetie darling. And yours."

Val muttered under her breath after Kim hung up. She understood that for most magazines ad revenue was tied to editorial content. If you wanted fast-food restaurants to advertise, you'd better have an article specifically mentioning that advertiser or at least French fries and burgers. It was even worse in so-called women's magazines. Ads for lip liner were invariably placed near articles on how to use lip liner or on the qualities of good lip liner which just happened to be the same qualities described in the ad. Her inner journalist was too pragmatic to be overly appalled.

She scrolled through her document one last time.

She found a few places to add brand names. She used *Sunrise*'s own recommended best buys as a source. At least then she knew she wasn't recommending junk.

My guests are almost here and it's lovely to greet them with a bank of beeswax candles in the foyer. It sets the mood for the evening and the light is wrinkle-friendly. Light, jazzy music drifts from the four speakers newly hidden in the living room. This project eliminated the speakers as boxy eyesores and the diagrams below will show you just how I did it.

Val's only stereo equipment was a boom box, but she had built the hidden speakers for someone else. Same thing. *Sunrise* had wanted Val to adopt Martha Stewart's personal style and so she had. It was actually easier for Val than the impersonal how-to articles she'd started with. It seemed to her that a reader would be more interested in reading about how to do something if they had a reason why.

Choose your speakers for their quality and size. They don't have to be identical. In particular, choose them with an idea as to where you're going to hide them. I chose a small Klipsch speaker because the diameter of the woofer was two inches less than the depth of the bookcase I was going to hide it in. My matching mahogany end tables hide a matched pair of Sonys. But don't forget you need the means to balance the sound between speakers so a large speaker doesn't drown out the others. An investment in a good quality receiver might be necessary to pull this project off. (See Aug '97 p. 98 for Consumer Electronics Special Report for Best Buys tips on receivers). Infra-red hookups, though expensive, can eliminate wiring worries completely.

She wasn't crazy about the brand name thing, but if she stayed with good quality and generally available merchandise she knew she wasn't leading anyone astray. She mentally constructed the speaker hideaways as she proofed the article for the last time, then skimmed the closing paragraph.

Music and a menu should complement each other. Jazz calls for light and sparkling fare. Simple ingredients handled with care can make a fine feast. Grapes rinsed with spring water and splashed with champagne for Louis Armstrong. Mashed sweet potatoes with honey as an artichoke dip for Chet Baker. Art Tatum? Chicken Marsala and giant sweet cheese ravioli with blanched sugar-snap peas. Dave Brubeck? That's easy — Napa Valley Chardonnay shimmering in crystal. If food be the music of love, dine on.

Shakespeare, the hack, would forgive her. She e-mailed the finished article, then settled into her well-worn comfy chair, avoiding the broken spring out of habit. She dug through the magazines stacked on the floor to find the *Architectural Digest* article on poured concrete flooring. She found it, eventually, behind the crate she used as an end table.

She wondered for a few minutes about heading to

happy hour where the girls were always aplenty. No, she needed an early night if she was going to look her best for the video shoot in the morning. Her nose was swelling slightly and sleep was the best way to help that. Any activity that required breathing through her nose for any length of time was right out. She hadn't done any heavy breathing for over five months now. All plastic surgeons should be shot.

VAL: The next step in this process is simple, but messy. Let's see how Janice is coming along. (*to door behind you*)

JAN: Well, Val, I'm just about ready to pour the grout solution on our tile counter.

VAL: Nice duds.

JAN: (*laughs*) I learned the hard way to wear a slicker and boots working with liquid grout.

VAL: (*to camera*) This solution is easy to mix and pour. It can even be tinted to shades more complimentary to your tile color.

(*chit chat/pour/and out*)

VAL: (*to camera*) We're going to leave this to set while we check on Stan's progress with the bathroom flooring.

"Cut!"

Jan clapped her hands. "That wasn't as hard as I thought it would be. I could get used to this TV stuff."

"The proof is in the tape." Val worked her jaw back and forth and then grimaced. Her face muscles felt as if they couldn't stop smiling. Her contacts stung, but her eyes were too dry to tear. She longed to take them out, but the contacts were the only way she could read the teleprompter. All the liquid in her body seemed to be in her nose. She sniffled.

"Your face could get stuck in that position." Mike cruised past her with his high-tech steady cam on his shoulder, leaving Val to lug the portable teleprompter.

"I'm afraid I'm going to end up like Sue Ann Nivens." Val trailed after Mike.

"Is Sue Ann your latest barfly?"

"Mike, you are so out of it. Sue Ann Nivens . . . the Happy Homemaker . . . the *Mary Tyler Moore Show* . . . television. Is any of this ringing a bell?"

"Television. What a waste of time."

Val rolled her eyes at Stan, who was setting up the bathroom shot. "This from a man who is supposed to help me get famous. I'm doomed." Belatedly, she realized she should have argued with Mike's innuendo that Val was over acquainted with barflies.

Stan grunted as he whacked the underlaying down in one corner. "I've known that from the beginning."

"You never know," Val began optimistically, but then she had to laugh. "I'm doomed."

But she hoped her shared investment in good equipment for Mike to do the filming would give her a professional quality demo tape. It was cheaper than hiring a pro, that was for sure. Pitching her own show would be easier with proof that she could perform in front of a camera. It hadn't been hard to convince Mike to do the filming. He was practicing shooting outdoors and lighting and wanted some money for better equipment. He was good enough at it that Val hardly cared that he couldn't name a single Brady.

Not even Marcia. He'd also known friends working on a small construction project — Jan and Stan appeared to be getting a kick out of being filmed. The homeowner had agreed, too, even though it meant that the day's work wasn't as productive as usual, but it was only for one day.

They worked steadily until the light began to fade, then Mike packed up. He promised them all professional dubs of the tape, then disappeared down the rutted track to the road.

"I'm starved."

Val started. Jan's voice in her ear had taken her by surprise. "So am I. Is that steakhouse in town any good?"

"Don't know. Feel up to an adventure?"

Vibes. Val was getting good vibes from Jan. She had thought Jan and Stan Marsh were husband and wife. Now she realized they both had the same slightly bent nose and high forehead. Brother and sister. Well, alrighty then.

"Sure. Lead the way."

She followed Jan's Toyota into the outskirts of Healdsburg and decided that Jan's long legs and quirky smile were endearing. Certainly worth getting to know. Highway 101 was clogged heading north from San Francisco, but the southbound journey was easy enough.

The steakhouse was crowded, giving them time to down beers and attempt conversation over the bar babble. Val learned that Stan and Jan were indeed siblings, and that Stan was also "family."

"He said you were cute," Jan shouted in Val's ear.

"Typical man." Val had to lean back awkwardly

around a pole at the bar to get into Jan's audible range. "Who wants to be cute?"

"I'd settle for cute. But you're . . . not cute."

Val grinned. "Thanks."

Jan's eyes sent a You're Welcome as she took her time assessing Val's not-cute qualities. Five months, Val thought. She was really enjoying this even though she was out of practice.

By the time they had eaten, neither making any bones about being hungry after the day's labor, Val was very conscious of Jan's knee pressing against hers under the table. They were sitting far closer than the size of the booth warranted. When the waiter offered dessert and coffee Jan declined.

"We could take in a movie if you like," Jan suggested.

Val nodded to make the waiter go away, then said with a quirk of her lips she couldn't suppress, "A movie is not quite what I had in mind."

Jan's eyes half-closed and Val heard her catch her breath. The booth was not nearly dark enough to do what she wanted, which was to kiss Jan thoroughly, and damn the consequences to her sinuses.

"Did you notice the motel across the street?"

Val nodded. She let her knees part as Jan's hand slid slowly between her thighs.

"Why don't you get us a room," Jan whispered, her palm firmly against the seam of Val's jeans, "and I'll get breakfast."

"It's a deal." Her hips tilted to give Jan more access. They did it all by themselves. Val's ability to make conscious decisions was fast slipping away.

They left the restaurant at a slow walk. Each step

felt like foreplay — the sound of Jan's thighs rubbing together, the light brush of Jan's shoulder against hers. As they crossed the motel parking lot Val took advantage of a patch of shadow to put her arm around Jan.

"Wait for me right here," she said. She didn't want to be too abrupt, but she couldn't help but give in to the urge to brush her lips across Jan's neck and earlobe.

Jan was obviously not feeling very patient either. She hummed her pleasure and slipped her hands under Val's sweater.

Val's nuzzles turned quickly to half-biting kisses as she worked her way to the hollow of Jan's throat. She went weak-kneed when Jan's fingertips deftly found and encouraged Val's swelling breasts.

"You want this, don't you?" Jan's question required no words. Val's body answered in quivering yesses.

She tore herself away from the delicious attention Jan was paying to her breasts only when she knew she had two choices — get a room or do it on the ground.

She was back as quickly as possible and they stumbled toward the room. Jan's jeans were unbuttoned and Val's bra undone by the time they got the door unlocked and stumbled through it. Val kicked it shut as Jan pulled her to the floor.

They didn't make it to the bed right away.

They went right to what they needed. Jan shoved Val's sweater out of the way and feasted on the swollen flesh of Val's breasts. Val shuddered and bit back an unnecessary plea, then groaned with delight

as her hand finally made its way past too much cloth
and buttons to the heat of Jan's clasping thighs.

She slid her fingers through Jan's shuddering
wetness and offered up her breasts for all the
attention Jan wanted to give them. It was hard to
concentrate. The part of her that controlled her
fingers was losing focus.

Jan gasped. "Hurry."

"Hold still for a moment," Val managed to say, but
Jan ignored her. Val managed to tear her breasts away
from Jan's mouth and get enough of a grip on Jan's
jeans to pull them down. She slid under Jan until she
could curve her hand inward.

Jan froze as Val entered her, then ground herself
onto Val's fingers. "Jesus. How did you get me like
this?"

Val could have asked the same question. She was
aching for the same delicious treatment she was giving
Jan.

Jan's orgasm was sudden and convulsive. Val
wrapped her legs around Jan's thigh, bringing the
energy of Jan's shaking against her own need.

Jan finally rolled off her onto the floor. "Jesus."

"I assure you, he's got nothing to do with it."

"Shaddup," Jan said, her voice edged with
fondness.

Val raised herself up on one elbow and shared a
smile with Jan in the dim light from the window.
Then, knowing that Jan was watching, she brought
her hand, covered with Jan's essence, and slowly ran
her tongue along her index finger. She felt drunk on
sex, and it was a fantastic feeling after five long
months without even a kiss.

Jan said huskily, "You can get that right from the source."

"I should tell you that I —" Val began. That wasn't the right way to go about it. "I haven't had a chance to, I mean I have, well, there's a chance that, I guess I'd say I don't know if — shit." She slumped on the floor. She congratulated herself for having thoroughly ruined the mood.

"Are you trying to tell me you've never done this before?"

"Not with this nose." *Val, you idiot. You know she's going to laugh.*

Jan laughed. And why wouldn't she? "Well, I suppose a new nose could make certain things different."

"I have a temporary condition," Val admitted miserably. "At least I hope it's temporary. I can't really breathe through my nose for any long period of time." She really didn't want to belabor this. *Why didn't I just do it and make the best of it?*

"I suppose you've never had sex with a head cold."

Val's sense of humor reasserted itself. "Head colds only stick around for seventy-two hours. They drink all the milk and don't bring their own Kleenex. Lousy lovers."

Jan tickled her, then suggested they move to the bed. She shed the rest of her clothes and lounged on the sheets with her body accessible from every angle. "I don't care if it takes you all night to reperfect your technique."

Val hid a nervous swallow as she pulled her sweater over her head, kicked her shoes off, and shinnied out of her jeans. She straddled Jan's bare thigh. "Maybe I need a refresher course before I give it a try."

Jan sat up and drew Val's mouth to hers for a sensuous kiss. Her lips descended to chin, to jaw, to throat.

"Please," Val whispered. She lifted her breasts to Jan's mouth, then threw her head back in surrender. She was soon on her back and ecstatically aware that she'd forgotten nothing about what it felt like to be with a woman.


"It seems to me," Jan said, after Val had recovered her composure, "that you just spent a long time breathing very hard through your nose."

"I did?" Val thought about it. Paper-thin apartment walls had taught her to clamp her mouth shut when she wanted to scream. Jan was right. A slow smile spread over her face. Her sinuses were just fine — she should have tried this sooner. "Well then, come here, woman."

"I intend to," Jan said. She put her hand on the nape of Val's neck, lightly massaging the taut muscles. Val purred her approval, then let Jan pull her head down.


Jan was so upfront about having enjoyed Val's company for the night that Val was only the teensiest bit annoyed when Jan made it very clear that there were no emotional strings attached — Jan was stealing her lines. But they did agree to call each other. It had been too good not to.

Back in her apartment Val settled in for an afternoon of reading, glad that no one was around to see the silly smile she couldn't stop. It was good to know she was fit as a fiddle and ready for love. Plastic surgeons no longer needed to be shot. Yesterday's gray skies had given way to blue and she pushed the sofa over into the sunlight and stretched out like a cat.

She woke up ravenous and in a panic because she heard a strange voice in her apartment. A woman's voice. After a moment she realized it was the answering machine.

"So let's have a weekend, okay? Ever been up the coast at all? We could dine out and sleep in." Jan laughed.

Val scrambled for the phone. "I was asleep," she confessed.

"Funny, I needed a nap this afternoon, too. Then I got to thinking about why and decided to call you."

"I'd love to go away for the weekend. Which one?"

"Weekend after next. Do you want to stay someplace romantic and cozy or —"

"Someplace with thick walls."

Jan chortled. "You read my mind, you wicked girl."

"Do we have to wait until then to see each other?"

"I have a family thing to do next weekend. Sorry."

Val sighed. Well, she'd gone without for many moons, so two weeks was a piece of cake. Besides, she had her own work to do. "We'll just have to make the most of it, then."

"I could make a suggestive reply to that, but phone sex is really not my thing."

"Okay, I hear the sound of good-bye."

"Never good-bye, mah precious one," Jan oozed, in a thick French accent. "Just ta ta for now."

Val chiseled a box of macaroni and cheese out of the freezer and crossed her fingers while it microwaved that she wouldn't blow a fuse. She peered at the bubbling contents and decided it wasn't as old as she had thought. She burned her tongue on the first bite, then gobbled the rest.

She settled down in front of the computer for the evening to write the core of her next *Sunrise* article. Tomorrow she could go for a long walk in Golden Gate Park, then out to a renovation project she was overseeing for an absent owner. Monday she had two more appointments with agents. Maybe Mike would get her the demo tape in time for those meetings. If she kept at it long enough someone would take some interest. Surely someone would. Of course they would. Wouldn't they?

# Banana Pancakes

With thanks to the Queen of Pancakes, Liesel Hammond.

## BATTER:

| | |
|---|---|
| 1 Tbsp vegetable oil | 1 to 1-1/2 cups milk (nonfat okay) |
| 1 to 2 eggs or egg substitute | 1/2 tsp cinnamon |
| 2 to 2-1/2 cups baking mix | 1 medium banana, sliced |

## PREPARATION:

In a large mixing bowl beat together oil and eggs until a bit frothy. (2 eggs makes for very fluffy pancakes.) On low mixer speed add the baking mix (Bisquick™ or equivalent) and 1 cup of the milk and the cinnamon. Continue beating on low and add additional milk 2 tablespoons at a time until your batter is creamy but not runny. Remove mixer and fold in banana slices.

## METHOD:

Heat a square griddle on high for a minute or two, then reduce to medium and drip 1-2 big drops of oil on the surface. Heating the griddle first will help keep pancakes from sticking; the heat source should be in the center of the griddle. Smooth oil across griddle with a spatula. Re-oil the griddle after every two batches of pancakes. Test the heat of the griddle with a few droplets of water. If the water spatters, the griddle is hot enough. The griddle will retain more heat the longer you cook, so you may have to turn it down as you go.

Drop batter in big spoonfuls in the four corners at least 1/2" to 1" apart. Try to get only one or two banana slices in each spoonful. If the cakes run together, the batter is too runny. Throw them out and add a heaping spoonful of baking mix to the remaining batter and gently mix. If the batter doesn't flatten out at all it's too thick; throw them out, add a spoonful of milk and remix.

Pancakes are ready to flip when the bubbling edges begin to look dry. If you wait until the center looks dry your pancake will be overcooked. A second spatula can be helpful to steady the pancake as it's lifted. Once flipped, press on the pancake gently to ensure even browning on the bottom. If the pancake has circular rings on it, you used too much oil or left the oil in puddles. If the pancake stuck, you didn't use enough oil. If it's cooked through, but too dark, turn the heat down a touch; too light turn the heat up and leave it a bit longer before flipping next time. Be sure to scrape off all the droplets of pancake before you pour the next batch or they will burn.

The bananas will be very hot, so be careful! Serves 3 to 4 hungry people, adding jam, butter and syrup as they wish. Makes 16-20 pancakes.

### From the Waterview, Mendocino

# 3

The first glimpse of the small town perched atop the gray-green headlands brought fresh tears to Jamie's eyes. She willed them away. She wanted to have some semblance of equanimity when she saw Liesel.

The whitewashed buildings were dazzling in the late-afternoon sun. Offshore, a tall bank of fog waited for its moment to blanket the town in quiet, sending the tourists back to their lodgings or into one of the half-dozen restaurants. She turned off Highway 1 onto Lansing Street. When she passed Union she didn't turn, but instead continued down the slope of the headland toward the bluffs. When she turned off the engine the first thing she heard was the low lament of the foghorn.

KatzinJam wandered away from the car to do some private cat business, but Jamie stayed in the car for some time, watching the sun drop behind the fog. In a single moment the bright afternoon dimmed to early evening, and the wind curling through her open window snapped cold against her cheeks. Aunt Emily had loved that moment. How many times had she stopped everything she was doing to step out onto the porch with her coffee to feel the day reclaimed by the relentless pattern of coastal weather? Poor Liesel, she thought suddenly. Another afternoon over and she's all alone.

Mendocino was too far from San Francisco for a casual visit. Distance, and a ten-hour work day six days a week, had kept her from visiting Aunt Em since her return from Philadelphia last year. Since deciding to leave Mendocino for cooking school she'd only returned once, over two years ago, and the inevitable meeting with Kathy had damaged her self-esteem so much she just couldn't risk it again, not until she'd done something, made her mark, anything that helped her hold her head up under the torment of Kathy's flaying tongue. She wondered if learning to cope with Marcus would help. She was sure to meet Kathy if she stayed in Mendo for any length of time.

She'd written Aunt Em weekly — sometimes more often. She sent her a videotape the school made of her class. Aunt Em mentioned Kathy only in passing in her letters. She knew why Jamie stayed away so long. In one letter Aunt Em sent a recipe for *spanakoppita*, noting, with a touch of wistfulness, that she hadn't made it in thirty-five years because it reminded her too vividly of her first love. All wounds heal, she'd written, but they do take time. Jamie had wondered then if she was trying to comfort her. Most likely. And what a letter writer Aunt Em had been. Almost a lost art in an electronic world.

Her thoughts wandered as she watched the mist gain its first inch of rocky land. As it crept toward her car she inhaled the salty aroma on the wind and let the sound of seagulls and waves fill her ears. She was home. It had been too long.

KatzinJam was gnawing on Jamie's overnight bag by the time Jamie pulled up in front of the house Aunt Em and Liesel had shared after selling the Waterview. Liesel had two cats, so Jamie assured Katz there was food forthcoming.

Liesel opened the door before Jamie was halfway up the walk, her arms spread in greeting. They wrapped around Jamie with a fierceness that warmed Jamie's aching heart.

"I knew you'd come," Liesel whispered in her ear. "She wanted it this way. I wanted to call you, but she wanted it this way." The rest was lost in a rush of heartfelt German that Jamie half understood from Liesel's early attempt to make her bilingual.

They sat over Delft blue demitasses of Liesel's incredibly strong coffee. Liesel welcomed KatzinJam, told Hansel and Gretel to be friendly, and set KatzinJam in front of the food dish. Jamie was amazed that the three animals didn't even spit at one another, but Liesel had that effect on animals and people. On everyone but Kathy, actually.

Jamie had never been in the house, but the cups,

the table, the linens, the aroma of chicken broth from the familiar stockpot on the stove, the jolt of the coffee on her nerves — they were all home. She felt parts of her filling up that she hadn't realized were empty. But the biggest emptiness, she knew, would remain.

"It was her pancreas. The cancer was there. Do you remember when she was ill last winter?" Jamie nodded. Liesel's rolling *R* was delightful to hear. "That was when they found it. She was having that chemotherapy and after two months of not being able to keep a spoonful of anything in her stomach for more than an hour she stopped going. She had lost thirty-five pounds — imagine that."

It was hard to imagine. Aunt Em had been a large woman, broad-shouldered and tall. Rubenesque, Liesel had always said. Still, thirty-five pounds would have left her gaunt. "But the picture she sent, she looked wonderful."

Liesel was nodding. "Yes, as soon as she stopped that chemotherapy she felt better. She hadn't felt ill before it, but the doctors said go, so she went. But when they looked again, after the two months, they said there was no improvement and with the treatments she would live perhaps eighteen months. Without it, probably not even a year. She said she wasn't going to make her last months of life an agony. She stopped going and felt much better for quite a while."

"I wish she'd told me."

"You were just settling into your life. She didn't want you to give it all up to worry over her. I think she was afraid you'd try to convince her she should go back for treatments."

"I might have." Jamie sipped the coffee and let it zigzag through her nerves. The way Liesel made it should be illegal.

"When she began to feel ill it happened very quickly. She was worse every day. It happened so fast. I expected it, but I was still stunned when she . . ." Liesel bowed her head over her cup.

"I know." Jamie patted Liesel's hand. "Don't relive it, *liebchen*."

They sat in silence while the dusk turned to night. Liesel stirred, finally, saying, "I've made some dumpling soup. I knew you would be here today. It will only take a few minutes to finish."

Dumplings . . . oh my. Liesel's dumplings floated on broth in defiance of gravity. Jamie set the table, automatically falling into the routine of life before she had left home. One of the first things Aunt Em had taught was that a set table was a sign of civilized behavior. Liesel ladled the rich soup into thick stoneware bowls patterned with delicate wildflowers — wildflowers Jamie had looked at every day of her life since arriving in Aunt Em's home.

Like the German chocolate cookies, the soup was incredibly comforting. Liesel was more of a gossip than her aunt had been, so Jamie caught up on what was behind a divorce Aunt Em had mentioned and shared Liesel's outrage that a new merchant was petitioning to widen Lansing Street to four lanes.

The bed Liesel tucked her into, just as if Jamie were twelve again, was the one she'd always known, from the room on the third floor that had been hers. She could almost smell Aunt Emily's apple cobbler in the oven and hear the scratchy Louis Armstrong recordings that had often brightened an evening.

KatzinJam curled up as close as possible to the middle of the bed and before she would have thought possible, Jamie was asleep.

Banana pancakes greeted her in the morning and Jamie heeded Liesel's advice to visit old stomping grounds and see if she could find Jacob O'Rhuan, who had disposed of Aunt Em's ashes.

Jacob was easy to find. When Jamie opened the front door, he was on the steps.

"Come away in," Liesel called from the kitchen.

"I thought you'd be here," Jacob said in his booming voice. "Do I smell pancakes, m'darling?"

Jamie let herself be drawn back into the house and even ate another pancake while Jacob downed six or seven.

"She told me I'd know where a good place was, and she was right. I automatically went out to my favorite place to watch the tide. Where you can see the town but not the cars and people. Nice place." He forked the last bite of pancake into his mouth, chewed thoughtfully and added, "I've got a tourist charter tomorrow. If you crew for me I'll take you by."

"I'd love to," Jamie said quickly. She hadn't been on the water for years.

Jacob smiled, his beard bristling where deep-cut laugh lines pulled tight. He'd been Aunt Em's friend for over forty years, had wanted to marry her after her husband died. But Aunt Em had known by then that friendship was all she needed from men. Jacob had been a little suspicious of Liesel Hammond when she'd become part of Aunt Em's life, but that had mellowed into lasting friendship, too. It all would have been idyllic if Liesel had lived with them, but Kathy had made that impossible.

"I've been hearing," Jacob added, "that you've gone and got yourself a fancy culinary degree."

Jamie shook her head. "No degree. Just lots of classes."

"And you been putting any of it to good use? I'm thinking I could use a good caterer in town again for the charters. Hasn't been the same since Em stopped filling my orders. The Waterview sure hasn't been the same either. Liesel here is a fine cook —"

"But dumplings and pancakes are my limit. I'll never have Em's imagination or her way with pie crust." Liesel turned quickly to the stove.

"I don't know how long I'll be staying," Jamie said into the awkward silence.

"Well, now, Liesel will be wanting you here."

Liesel plopped one last pancake on Jacob's plate, serene once more. "We haven't even had a chance to talk about it. My door is always open to you, sweetling. Always will be and for as long as you need it."

"Well, I have a job." A job she was growing to hate. "But Em left me her money, you know that, right?"

Liesel sat down and fixed Jamie with a no-nonsense stare. "As it should be. You were more of a daughter to her than — I can't even say her name. I never told Em just how I felt about Kathy because it wouldn't have served any purpose. She's a bitch of the first order and I'm glad she won't benefit a dime. You do what you want. I did my twenty in the Army, and I've got all I'll ever need."

Jamie swallowed hard, aware that if Liesel hugged her she'd cry again. She blinked furiously to keep the tears back. Kathy *was* a bitch of the first order, but

45

that didn't change Jamie's lingering regrets or the if-onlies she played in her head when she was lonely. She was aware that Jacob was querying Liesel with a glance and that Liesel gave a slight shrug in response.

Jacob set his coffee cup down with a thud. "Well, how about you throw something together for me tomorrow? I've got about seventy dollars to spend on sodas and snacks for twelve. Nothing really fancy, but tasty counts."

"Okay," Jamie found herself saying. It would be something to do. And crewing would be a blast. "How about crab puffs and finger fruits and vegetables, and some rolled sandwiches?"

"Sounds delicious, m'darling." Jacob counted out the cash and winked. "I'm assuming you'll be keeping enough of that to cover your time. And there's the usual crew pay tomorrow. Jeff'll be there, too."

"I'd love to see him again. Thanks."

Jacob drained his third cup of Liesel's coffee — which would keep him awake for three days, Jamie thought. She had missed the squeak of his slicker and boots. The screen door slammed behind him.

"That man could wake the Titans," Liesel said fondly.

"His heart is as big as his voice."

"I don't want to push you, Jamie, but think about what you want to do. I know it was a lot of money Em left you." She took Jamie's hand. "She longed to know you were happy."

Jamie squeezed Liesel's fingers, noticing the extra wrinkles and spots that had come over the years. "I know. But I don't think I know yet what will make me happy. I just know what won't."

Liesel let go of her hand with a sigh. "She won't

ever change. She's marrying that big-shot lawyer. What a donkey's behind he is."

Liesel had always been the repository of Jamie's turmoil over Kathy. She just hadn't been able to tell Aunt Em much more than the basics. She loved Kathy. Kathy didn't love her. "I don't believe she'll change. I just wish I could put it behind me."

"Well, you just take a breather here for a while, then. Things will seem much clearer after you get the city air out of your lungs."

Jamie grinned, suddenly lighthearted. "I think you're right about that. And I think I'll go for a walk, like you suggested."

"Call if you won't be back for lunch. I was thinking of turning out some sour cream biscuits."

Jamie was at the door, but she rushed across the kitchen to give Liesel a bear hug. "I will stay, if only for your biscuits."

"Don't make promises yet, it's too soon. Now get on with you."

The fog peeled back as Jamie walked up Union Street toward Lansing. She peeked into stores and when she saw a familiar face she went in for hugs and condolences — she had missed the genuine human warmth of the small town. Her aunt had been well-regarded and each embrace felt like a loving tie being wrapped around her heart. She would stay because this was home. And Kathy be damned. She couldn't let Kathy make her stay away anymore. She'd already cost her the last years of Aunt Em's life. It would be a long time before she forgave Kathy — or herself — for that.

Her footsteps lead her unerringly toward the Waterview. The old inn faced Main Street, a few doors down from the much more splendid Mendocino Hotel. Aunt Em hadn't wanted the fuss of daily check-ins and maid service, so the inn was really a boardinghouse for seasonal workers, with a full scale eatery on the ground floor. Aunt Em preferred calling it an eatery because her food was simple, inexpensive and plentiful. It was the kind of place where two dollars on the counter brought you an endless cup of coffee and a slice of pie, with some change left for the waitress.

Well, that's how it had been. Jamie peered through a dirty window and saw that her aunt's scrubbed wood tables topped by glass had been replaced by fancy black lacquer. A chichi neon sign read "Dining Room." The menu on the wall was gone and she saw a waitress — could that be Darlene? — handing a tasseled gold card to a diner.

The dinnerware and food coming from the kitchen looked the same, though. Maybe the new owner had thought some frills would bring in more customers. She glanced at the menu in the holder outside — yikes. Coffee and pie would cost five bucks. No wonder the place was sparsely filled, even though early lunch was approaching. Sure it was offseason and the tourist trade was just a trickle. But there was no one she recognized inside except Darlene. Local customers had kept Aunt Em going. Tourist season was a bonus with more than enough extra trade from folks grateful for a no-frills meal that helped out the budget.

For that kind of money you could be at the posh Mendo Hotel, or over at McCallum House. The dinner prices were almost what the world-famous Café Beaujolais, just up the street, commanded. Her aunt had never tried to compete with the haute cuisine in Mendocino — it was too good.

Jamie slipped through the front door to catch Dar's eye when she finished with her customer.

"Jamie, sweetie, you're a sight for sore eyes." Dar's hug was the biggest of the day, so far. She had worked for Aunt Em for years and had apparently carried over to the new regime. "I'm so sorry about Em, but I have to tell you it was a relief. She was in such a bad way, I'm glad she was finally released. Come have a cup, no, you're drinking Liesel's, how about some soda or water? Sit over here, sweetie, the counter's gone, I miss it."

Jamie took the seat Dar indicated and smiled inwardly, remembering how Dar's voluble nature had sold slices of pie by the dozen.

Dar dropped her voice. "I won't suggest you have anything to eat. It's overpriced and doesn't hold a candle to anything Em turned out. Don't know where Bill found this cook — second one in four months. Bill's in the back, he says I gab too much. Be right back."

Jamie watched as Dar delivered a check, filled three coffee cups and cleared away plates. As she took the dishes to the kitchen Jamie could tell the meals were half-eaten, and from what she saw she didn't blame them. Burnt burgers and canned vegetables. The fries looked like dough.

Dar set a piece of pie in front of her. "Thought you'd want to see what they have the nerve to call Emily's Special." She whisked away to deliver a check.

Jamie took a bite and put the fork down with a shudder. It was canned cherry pie filling on a store-bought frozen crust. Nothing wrong with the crust, really, but it needed a special filling to compensate for the lack of flakiness. The topping was decent, with small bits of coconut, but it didn't save the pie from mediocrity. Aunt Em would have been mortified if anyone thought the recipe was hers. Jamie wondered how the new owner was staying afloat.

A man with a deep scowl peered out from the kitchen. He saw Jamie looking and faked a genial smile. "Welcome," he boomed.

Dar went back to the kitchen, saying as she breezed by, "Bill, this is Jamie Onassis, Emily Smitt's niece."

"Jamie, well, it's a pleasure," Bill said. "I really admire the way your aunt ran this place. If I do it half as well I'm a happy man."

Jamie made polite noises, lied about liking the tables and asked how business was.

"I wish I could say it was doing better. I had to move folks out to do some renovating and so far no one has moved back. I just found out my sister is ill and wish I could go help her out, but you know how being a small-business owner is. Vacation means no income and I'm stretched pretty tight."

Aunt Em had always been able to leave the place for a couple of weeks a year, having loyal, solid employees to look after it. Offseasons she'd closed on Mondays, too. "Mind if I look around? I grew up here and I'm curious what you've done."

"Sure. Nice to have you back in town."

Yeah, right, she thought. Bill's joviality didn't fool her. His business was failing. She looked around the kitchen and it was easy to see the signs. At least one stove was no longer in working order, and all of the other appliances looked like the ones her aunt had owned. Business was so slow that only one refrigerator was even turned on, and the big walk-in was empty.

The back stairs were depressing — carpet falling to pieces, dirty paint. The second floor had had eight small bedrooms sharing two baths. It looked like Bill had tried to put two rooms together and capture one of the baths in that room for some sort of suite. The work was half-finished and what was done was poorly executed. Jamie didn't know how to hang wallpaper, but she could tell when a pattern wasn't matched.

No wonder none of the regulars had come back. Six people to one bathroom? Jamie was willing to bet Bill had raised the rent, too.

She briefly visited the top floor, taking in the view of the headlands to the south. A million-dollar view of waves on rocks. Nothing up there seemed changed. One large bedroom had its own bath — it had been Aunt Em's. The two smaller rooms shared the other bath. Kathy's on the right, hers on the left. The rooms were empty of furniture but full of memories. Those first early years she had Kathy had sneaked into each other's rooms at night, two peas in a pod. The summer they were sixteen everything had changed, and not for the better.

She left after Dar confided that she thought Bill was behind on his mortgage payments and had even held up her paycheck for a couple of days last week. He obviously didn't have the skills or tenacity for running that kind of business, or had assumed, as so many newcomers in Mendocino had, that the tourist trade lasted longer than just the summer.

She was back at Liesel's in time for lunch, her head full of plans and wondering if she had the daring

51

to go through with them. She had the money; she had this open space in her life. She'd spent the last few years letting go of the past and what she needed to do was get on with living before she lost any more time.

"If we just do this between ourselves, well, then I'd save a whole lot of money on a broker's fee. I'd split the savings with you." Bill was giving her an open-eyed honest look that didn't fool Jamie.

She'd been to the recorder's office and knew what Bill had paid Aunt Em for the place, including the fixtures. He'd let it run down substantially, and there was little left of the goodwill Aunt Em had built up. "Sounds fine to me. I'm interested in saving money. There's a lot of improvements to make here. I've got a standard purchase agreement here that's valid in California. All you need to do is sign."

Bill went rabid when he saw her offer — sixty percent of what he'd paid, but all of it in cash within the week. Liesel and Jacob had counseled her not to rush into things, but Jamie wanted the Waterview, and didn't want Bill to put it on the open market. She hoped that the offer of quick cash would seal the deal.

After an hour of wrangling, it did. Bill confessed it was enough to settle his mortgage and other trade debts and leave something for his old age, as he called it. Jamie knew he wasn't telling her everything, but she'd been in a lot of restaurants and had an idea what bringing the inn back to working condition would cost. With a little luck she would have enough. She was confident that once folks knew Em's niece was now running the place they'd give her a try, and she didn't plan to disappoint them.

Bill signed the purchase agreement while Jamie hid her shivers of exhilaration and terror. Jeff, Jacob's son, had told her flat out she was nuts not getting the place inspected first. Maybe she was. But she'd spent yesterday on the ocean for the first time in years, walked through the town after dark in fog that made San Francisco seem perpetually sunny, and had her first taste of Mendocino ice cream in ages. Home — this was home. She missed Aunt Em fiercely but every moment made her feel close again.

Maybe the Waterview needed a fresh coat of paint, and some repairs to the appliances. She didn't have to start off with a huge menu, just a good one. She could do this. Aunt Em would have wanted her to. So what if she broke out into a cold sweat when she drew the cashier's check at the bank? So what if Bill had taken it, signed the grant deed in front of the notary, and had his car already packed to leave town? How bad could it be?

# Christmas on the Coast

by Valkyrie Valentine

What do you remember about good holidays? Laughter, friends, family? Me, too. My memories also hold two very potent symbols of the holidays: smells and tastes. The scent of pine and cedar. Here on the coast is the tang of eucalyptus, which is even stronger when it's damp or foggy. The aroma of baking apples, sage in the turkey stuffing. All these smells make me think of good times. Try an evergreen bough in the living room and ginger and cinna[...] bubbling in a teap[...] stove—instant wa[...] memories.

And tastes of col[...] meals stay in my[...] Pumpkin, for one[...] pumpkin make you t[...] anything but wint[...] neither. Apple cider[...] cranberries, chestnu[...] peppermint ice crean[...] love the holidays!

One thing that ruins[...] holidays is stress. If[...] want to spruce up the house but have no time and less money, keep it simple! A wainscoting project can be done in an afternoon if you plan ahead. Peasant's wainscoting is two colors of paint and a strip of stained moulding—no need to learn to wallpaper with guests arriving! You only need one paint color if you like the existing color on the wall. I'm fond of wainscoting in rooms that do double and triple duty as offices, sewing rooms[...] rooms and [...]oms tend [...] any heavy [...] color will [...]ok even [...] project, [...]ll you're [...]ean and [...] Spackle [...] a tape [...]k the [...] your [...] people [...] about [...]hes off the floor. Make a pencil mark every

Mulled cider is easy and smells great on the stove. Just add whole allspice and cinnamon sticks to apple cider. Add some orange juice if you want. The beauty of mulled cider is you can fiddle and taste and modify to your taste and it becomes your recipe. The important thing is to enjoy your guests and your holidays. If you don't have fun, no one else will either.

# 4

It was the second week of November and I had flown into New York from Texas that morning to snatch five minutes with my father at corporate headquarters. I had to hurry to catch up after the staff meeting for *Sunrise* magazine broke up. This idea I'd had, ever since I'd met Valkyrie Valentine, wouldn't wait any longer. I couldn't wait any longer.

Even in pumps I passed most of the milling crowd and made it to the private elevator just as he and his entourage stepped in. "Daddy, wait up!"

His eyebrows shot up. We'd agreed on a measure

of decorum in public. I even used my mother's maiden name in business to keep a little of the nepotism charges at bay. "Ms. Thintowski," he intoned. He's got a great, deep voice which turns freshly minted M.B.A.s to pudding.

The damage was done, so I decided to let everyone think my business with him was personal, hence the informality. A quick kiss, a simple hug and a mention of yesterday's big win by one of the pro sports franchises he invested in, and he had forgiven me. He brought me a soda from the wet bar with his own two hands and shooed away his eager assistants.

I flopped down onto a couch in the south forty of the office, farthest away from the imposing solid mahogany desk. It was bigger than some dorm rooms and I really only liked the thing when I was behind it. He knew that and said it made him more sure than ever of my parentage.

"Daddy, I have an idea."

He looked amused. "Is that why you're wearing something other than Capri pants?"

He didn't much like my retro-'60s fashion choices. I liked them because very few women could wear them and look good. I'd forgone my usual beehive today, out of deference to my father's tastes. Even though a veritable team of technicians had tried to make me beautiful over the years, I'm rather plain if you look long enough. My physique, however, was as trim as a private trainer and steady devotion to exercise could make it. I could carry off the 1962 Chanel suit I was wearing. The spike heels on late '50s pumps are as comfortable to me as running shoes. Well, almost.

"I didn't want to embarrass you and I had

business to conduct anyway." I popped open the diet Coke. Nice of him to remember I'm Coke, not Pepsi.

"Did you know Marissa can't even open a soda? Or button her clothes?"

"Give me two minutes alone with her and a pair of nail clippers and the problem would be fixed." Marissa was girlfriend number four since daddy stopped marrying his girlfriends. "I don't know why you pick them so helpless."

"Because they're nothing like your mother."

I smiled. "Sweet."

"So this idea? I have a meeting in five minutes."

"Martha Stewart."

He looked confused, which meant he'd let his guard down. Not that I needed it down, but it always felt good to know that we still had a special relationship, one he didn't have with anyone else. Especially the girlfriends. "We do have five minutes, so you can explain more." He sat down, ready to indulge me by listening. Indulgence never had any effect on his business sense.

"Okay, Daddy. Martha Stewart. The one-woman arbiter of good taste and good living and one incredibly lucrative franchise. As you always say, competition is good. We need to find our own Martha Stewart. Someone we create and hold to a long-term contract to work for us. Not just one magazine, but us. Just think how easy it would be for you to simultaneously roll out a cable show, release a book, put her picture on the cover of a half-dozen magazines, while *Sunrise* headlines their exclusive column by our Martha Stewart." If the writer did to the public what she did to me, we were halfway there. My heart was going pitty-pat just recalling her devilish

57

smile. "Wouldn't you love to get some of the ad revenue that *Living* scoops up? Last issue had four pages of editorial before page forty — that's ninety percent ads."

He was shaking his head. "It's risky. She jumps ship after we make her a household name. It would be like Betty Crocker starting her own company after General Mills gave her the makeover."

"That's why I said long-term contract."

"Where would you find this paragon? You've got someone in mind, haven't you?"

"I do. She already writes for *Sunrise*." I handed him a sample column I knew would appeal to him.

"I should read my own magazines."

"You'd spend all your time trying to keep up. I understand why you stick to news. I happen to like reading about house kinds of stuff. And this column reminded me of — well, that last Christmas." He knew I meant the last one when Mom had been alive. We'd gone to Cape Cod. The details were like picture postcards in my mind.

He was reading it already. The article was called "Christmas on the Coast." Valentine had a good command of evocative detail. I could smell the cedar sprigs and mulled cider she described and even envision myself tackling wainscotting — that is, if I had any need to do it myself. Something about the way she wrote made me want to own a power drill.

Daddy handed back the article and stood up. "Do some more research, Sheila. It's time you ran something start to finish. I'm sure you'll bring me a winner."

His desk phone was buzzing and as he strode toward the desk I admired his vitality. Only after I turned thirty did I realize the degree to which he liked home and hearth. I wondered if he knew that his relationships didn't last because the women he attracted weren't homebodies and that they all fell rapidly out of love with him when they discovered he really did prefer romping with the dogs and hiking to shopping in Paris.

"I'll keep you up-to-date," I said from the door. "I've got two days free unexpectedly and I'll probably sound out this woman before I head for the shareholders' meeting. So I'll see you back in Dallas."

He rolled his eyes and reached for the phone. "I have the distinct feeling you haven't told me everything, but I can live with that." He winked, then said, "Mark Warnell," into the phone. I was dismissed.

As I shut the door behind me I wondered if the corporate jet was busy. What I hadn't told my father was how much of a hurry I was in to see Valkyrie Valentine in the flesh again. Very much in the flesh.



I loved the sound of her voice. Not husky, not breathy. Direct without being strident, right in the middle of the general female range in tone. She said hello and it made me shiver.

"Valkyrie Valentine?" I wondered, not for the first time, if that outlandish name was real. "This is Sheila Thintowski. I'm affiliated with *Sunrise*. I have an interesting proposal for you and wondered if we could meet over dinner this evening. It would be very much worth your while."

"How intriguing. Yes, I'm free for dinner."

"Good." I looked out the airplane window. If the

company jet had been available I'd have been on the ground already. *C'est la vie.* "It might be easier if I met you somewhere. I'll be coming from the airport." The sun was dropping behind a low bank of fog, streaking the skyscrapers with orange and red. I'm always surprised by how small the financial district of San Francisco looks, and how much water and green surrounds the city. So many trees. Everything from sailboats to ferries to cruise liners dotted the surface of the bay. Even the long lines of cars in stop-and-go traffic added glitter to the panorama.

"Why don't we meet at the Blue Muse on Hayes? At eight?"

"I'm sure a cabbie can find it. I look forward to seeing you again."

After a pause, she said curiously, "Have we met?"

"Yes. We shared a laugh over wine at the dedication of the new Hormel Center." The event had been very gay, in every sense of the word.

Her voice, incredibly, warmed even further. I could imagine it whispering seductive nothings in my ear. "I remember now. You told me to call you She-Thing."

"That's me."

"Well, I'm looking forward to seeing you later this evening then."

"See you at eight." I imagined her reclining on the delicate chaise of the reading room she'd described several issues ago. My imagination added that rich figure draped in silk, a slipper dangling from one slender foot. It had been a very long time since a woman had made me feel the way Valentine Valkyrie did. I intended to savor the feeling for years to come.

\* \* \* \* \*

The Blue Muse was a small restaurant with a fish pond. Not long on decor beyond the fish. I sipped a decent enough scotch at the bar while I waited. It was ten minutes after eight and even though I was eager to see Valentine again I was miffed at her late arrival. I was prepared to forgive her, however, given the proper inducement.

The door chime clinked and I looked in the mirror above the bar and this time it was her. Good God. Creamy skin brushed with bronze, ocean-blue eyes that made me want to dive into her depths. Could that color be real — I remembered them more violet — or was it tinted contacts? Let it be real, I thought, and her name, too. I wanted her to be real to me.

I slid off the barstool, sure that my miniskirt and matching bolero jacket, both in screaming chartreuse, would catch her attention. But as I approached she looked past me. That was two demerits. If it hadn't been for the way her red lips made it hard for me to concentrate I would have been truly piqued.

Then she looked at me, really looked at me. Our eye contact stilled us both for about five seconds, then someone else came in and we were approaching each other to shake hands, murmur polite greetings and pretend that we both weren't thinking where the nearest hotel was. At least, that's what I was thinking. Fortunately, my father's daughter waved red flags and I snapped out of my impulse to offer her anything for a smile.

I got plenty of smiles over dinner. Fresh Pacific salmon is a favorite of mine and the hollandaise was surprisingly spicy. She had medallions of filet mignon in a Roquefort sauce, and she ate every bite. The last three women I'd dated wouldn't eat a lettuce leaf between them for dinner, and her vibrant glow of health and lack of pretension made me feel, well, less jaded.

I couldn't tell you what we talked about before the coffee came. Whatever it was had been entertaining and stress-free.

She sipped her coffee, then cupped her chin in one elegant hand and fixed me with a warm, blue stare. "So I don't think you came all this way just to buy me dinner."

I would have, but perhaps on not so tight a schedule. "I wish I could say my intentions were that simple."

Her crimson lips curved in the soft light. "I doubt anything you do is simple."

"Well, I'll ask a simple question, then. Have you ever thought of doing a program in addition to your column?"

Her eyes lit up. Zing. "I have."

"Have you thought about how that could happen?"

"I can tell you how it won't happen. It won't happen with me knocking on agent's doors and pinholing executives at conventions."

I laughed. "You're right. What you need is someone who knows how it's done. And who thinks you are exactly what the house and home industry needs."

"And that would be you?" Her lips pressed together in a fixed smile and I realized I had no idea what she was thinking.

"That would be me. I've been reading your column for the last two years. After I met you in September I've been wondering just how you'd look on tape."

"I have a demo."

That caught me off guard. I don't know why I'd been hoping that the idea had only vaguely occurred to her. I wanted her to be a little ambitious, but Daddy was right — too much ambition and we could foot the bill for making her name a household word without building any loyalty to us. I kicked myself for my Svengali tendencies. "When could I see it?" I expected her say right now, at her apartment.

Instead she said, "I'll send it to you." Her color rose slightly and I wondered what the mystery was.

"I'd love to take it with me to show around at a shareholders' meeting."

Her dark, thick lashes hid her thoughts and made mine turn to less businesslike transactions. "I'm having it copied for a few people. I might be able to locate a copy tonight. Maybe I could drop it by your hotel so you could take it with you?"

"I'm not leaving until tomorrow afternoon." I had two appointments with ad agencies to fill out the trip. "But my day is rather full tomorrow. I'd love to see it tonight." A flash of blue told me she understood that I might have slightly more on my mind than the tape.

"Well, then, I'll have to get it to you tonight, won't I? It shouldn't be too hard."

"I'm glad you've given this some thought. I don't just work for *Sunrise*, I'm actually in the creative department for Warnell Communications." Her eyes widened. "And I know you appreciate how much Warnell could do for you."

"I do. And I know that you appreciate how much I could do for Warnell."

She certainly didn't lack confidence. Odd that I had flashes when I knew what she was thinking, but

63

mostly I hadn't a clue — she could surprise me. Okay, she didn't need a Svengali. Fine, I thought. A more equal partnership is more likely to last.

She was hailing a taxi when I remembered my curiosity about her name. I'd already ascertained that her eyes were that brilliant violet-green-blue — no sign of a lens. "I have to ask — your name?"

"Is it real?" She waved at a cab which sped on by. "Believe it or not, it is. Right on the birth certificate. Valentine isn't that rare a last name and my parents evidently thought it would be a hoot to call me Val Val." Those incredible eyes rolled heavenward. "Parents."

"Do you have a middle name?"

"Jeepers. Margaret. Do I look like a Margaret?"

I didn't think so, but I wasn't about to tell her I liked the name Margaret because my first serious lover had been a Margaret.

A cab coasted to the curb and she scooted in. I followed her, glad of the dark back seat, and not for the first time in my life. Unfortunately, my hotel was not very far away and only a few minutes later I paid the cabbie enough to take Val all the way home and we parted without so much as a kiss.

There was still later that night, I told myself.

At my hotel, satisfied with how my plans were progressing, I spent a few minutes asking myself if my libido was a good measure for the reaction of the American consuming public. Well, I liked beautiful women and lord knows the American appetite for them was insatiable. A beautiful woman who could build a house, cook a gourmet meal? For a huge segment of women, she'd represent an ideal. And men, being men, would wonder if all that energy and vibrant life would carry over to the bedroom. I laughed at myself. It wasn't just the men who would be wondering. Perhaps she'd even become a lesbian cult figure, like Xena.

My father had told me once that I never had a problem with small dreams.

I left voice mail for a marketing director I trusted to take me seriously about setting up focus groups. Then I called my favorite talent coordinator to do a profile of Ms. Valentine, warts and all. No sense thinking about market shares and syndication sales if she had something unpalatable in her past. I was prepared for an uphill battle against homophobia, but there was no sense making that job harder than it need be.

Another hour passed before my phone rang.

"I have a delivery for Sheila Thintowski," an unfamiliar voice announced. Egads, someone had a horrible head cold.

"Who is it from?"

"Uh, Valentine."

The cat! She had sent a messenger instead of coming herself! I looked down at my deceptively innocent flannel robe. More than one woman had thought the robe would never lead to bed, and they'd all been wrong. I sincerely believed, as Bette Davis did, that a bare shoulder emerging from flannel was more sexy than a naked body.

"Please give it to a bellman to be brought up. Can you get a message back to the sender?"

"Yeah." Usual slacker tones.

"Please tell her I'm disappointed we couldn't watch the tape together."

"Yeah, sure."

When the tape arrived I was sorely tempted to drop it out the window. She *had* been interested in me and yet had avoided an obvious opportunity to get to know me up close and personal.

Duh, I told myself. She just might be in an inconvenient relationship. Although she didn't seem the type. She had been too aware of me to be thoroughly invested with someone else. I was willing to bet she wasn't the monogamous type.

Well, maybe she didn't want to mix business and pleasure quite yet. After all, she had no idea who I was, not really. I could be just like any guy with casting couch intentions. I was certain she'd had her share of those offers. It rankled to think she might have thought that's what I had in mind. Maybe I had been a little over the top. Hmph.

Having nothing else more intriguing to do I watched the demo tape. The camera work was surprisingly good — she must have paid a pro. When it was over I was more certain than ever that my libido and business sense were both right on the money this time. Her informality and humor countered her beauty and elegance — she wouldn't threaten women. I was willing to predict quite a range of female demographics. Her competence and looks would pull in men.

I took the tape out of the machine and kissed it. It tasted like success.


Val rubbed her nose and prayed that Sheila had not recognized her voice. She was well aware that if she had gone up to Sheila's room she might have let her like of trim legs and full lips get the better of her. Sheila's goodwill could be the gift of a lifetime — or a curse.

She hurried out of the hotel, lest Sheila somehow discover her there, and splurged on another cab. A north wind chivied leaves and litter down Market Street, and she huddled inside her jacket. The events of the evening had left her more numb than the cold.

This Thintowski woman was pretty darned dynamic. It was quite obvious her intentions were both business and personal. She could do a lot for Val, and Val was quite certain that she would enjoy a personal relationship with She-Thing.

It wasn't until she had feared Sheila would ask where she lived that Val had realized she was in a bind. What she wrote in her columns about reading rooms and dens, foyers and fireplaces — it was all an amalgamation of other people's houses. Her apartment was a catastrophe. She couldn't entertain Sheila there. And what if Sheila stayed the night? Val knew her limitations. More than Pop-Tarts for breakfast and Sheila would know her cooking skills were . . . well, overstated. Fraud was such an unpleasant word.

She could see the value of Sheila's good opinion. Perhaps if they got further in negotiations, Val could come clean about her little exaggerations. But she had to hook Sheila. If she were someone else she could sleep with Sheila to cement their future, but it was not her style. Sex was for fun, not business, and not meant to use people. Besides, something warned her that Sheila wasn't one to let her emotions cloud her business judgment.

It was inconvenient to have a military father who had hammered into Val that anything earned easily wasn't worth having. The world did not come on a silver platter. Strong people made the platter themselves, then hauled the world onto it.

At home Val dithered about what she would do if Sheila called in the morning and wanted to see the wonderful home Val had been describing. Well, she would be out. But that wouldn't work for long. She wanted to meet with Sheila again because that was the only way to move forward.

The next morning Val used the answering machine to screen calls and went into a panic when she heard Sheila's voice.

"I think your demo tape is fabulous and I'll be making copies to send to a few people at Warnell. I was hoping to see you again before I left for a shareholders' meeting, but I had to reshuffle my appointments for today and leave a little earlier than planned. I'll be in touch with you early next week. I'd really like to see some of your projects. I'm partial to shrimp scampi — that's a big hint. I can't wait to taste your cooking." She rattled off a string of phone numbers where she could be reached and then hung up.

Thank God, Val thought. She was not ready for fame and fortune. Then she realized Sheila was expecting shrimp scampi when they did meet.

She packed for her weekend with Jan with a spinning head. Maybe she could claim that the house burned down. Maybe she could get the food from a restaurant. But Sheila would want to see her make it. And Sheila could never, ever see the apartment. Val didn't even know if the oven worked.

She met Jan downstairs. Jan had volunteered to do the driving and had taken care of all the arrangements, saying she knew the coast pretty well. Even though her thighs clenched at the sight of Jan, Val couldn't shake Sheila Thintowski, and all that Sheila could offer, out of her mind.

# Sauce for Cacciatore

This sauce is delightfully bright on chicken or grilled eggplant, or just as is over *al dente* pasta. It's also easy to make and leftover sauce freezes very well. It's just the sort of thing in the freezer that will feed unexpected guests in minutes.

1 3-ounce jar of marinated artichoke hearts
3 cloves garlic, minced
2 medium onions, chopped
4 carrots, bite-size chunks
4 stalks celery, sliced
2 red bell peppers, chopped
1/2 pound mushrooms (Portabello if available)
1 24- to 30-ounce can crushed plum tomatoes
1/2 tsp each dried oregano, salt, pepper
1 Tbsp dried basil

PREPARATION:

Chop and slice all vegetables. You can roast the red peppers if you like. Drain the marinade from the artichoke hearts into a 4-quart dutch oven.

METHOD:

Heat the artichoke marinade and sauté the carrots for 2-3 minutes, then add the garlic, onions, celery, peppers and mushrooms and sauté until thoroughly cooked and limp. Add all remaining ingredients and bring to a simmer for as little as 15 minutes or as long as 90 minutes. Simmering uncovered means a thicker sauce, but watch for sticking. Be sure to break up the artichoke hearts into bite-size pieces.

You can add a good quality red wine to the sautéed vegetables just before adding the other ingredients, particularly if the pan needs deglazing.

## Tip

If you decide to freeze some, add a tablespoon of lemon juice to the thawed sauce during heating to perk up the flavors. This trick works with a lot of frozen and canned sauces and soups.

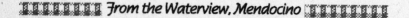 *From the Waterview, Mendocino*

# 5

Jan drove like a maniac up Highway 1. The scenic beauty of low gray mist over rolling blue ocean was lost on Val as she clutched the passenger grip and braced herself for every horseshoe turn. By the time they stopped in Jenner-by-the-Sea for lunch, Val was half exhausted. She kept thinking about the night ahead and its certain pleasures, but it was not balancing out a day of sheer terror.

By the time they arrived at a lesbian-run bed and breakfast in Little River, Val was ready to scream. Maybe she could volunteer for the drive back. Maybe she could take the bus back. When she stepped out of the car she wanted to kiss the ground.

They had a lovely dinner in nearby Mendocino, and that took the edge off of Val's certainty that she'd had a near death experience. The evening that followed, in their own little cabin behind the main house, made the drive up worth it — but Val still wasn't sure the about the drive back.

They spent Saturday morning in bed. Only desperate hunger got them up. They feasted on surprisingly good burgers in Mendocino, a town Val had always thought too upscale and holistic to sport a joint with burgers fried on the grill next to the bacon and onions. Afterwards, they explored the little shopping district, poking in and out of consignment shops, a neat-o keen toy store and dozens of boutiques with lots of local-made clothing, art and jewelry.

Val fell in love with one of the home craft stores. They had wrought-iron outdoor faucet handles in whimsical shapes — everything from a spotted ladybug to a winged fairy. The statuary made her want to start gardening immediately, incorporating an entire plan around a concrete bench fashioned with the front and hindquarters of a smirking pig as the two uprights.

Nevertheless, as taken as she was with Jan and the town, Sheila Thintowski continued to plague her. She didn't know how she was going to actually *be* the person Sheila obviously thought she was. Well, she was 80% that person. She just couldn't cook to save her life and, well, who cared if she didn't exactly live in the place she described? That she hadn't renovated a single place into a showpiece but rather done projects for other people? Some of those projects had been complex and expensive. Maybe Sheila would see the funny side of it. Yeah, right.

Sunday morning, while Jan was still asleep, Val bundled into her overcoat and walking shoes, left a note saying she'd be back with coffee and breakfast, and took the car back to Mendocino. The air was cold and wet — perfect for a solitary walk on the windswept headlands. She nodded to other people out strolling, but no one spoke. Something about the cold and ocean in the early morning light made talk unwelcome.

She tried to think through an approach to Sheila Thintowski, a way to explain herself without losing Sheila's respect. If there was a way she hadn't thought of it by the time she went back to the car. She drove up Main Street again and was chagrined to see almost nothing open at that hour. What had she expected? Starbucks? That would be sacrilege in a town that was still refreshingly unique.

An Open sign caught her eye and she pulled up to the wooden sidewalk in front of a place called the Waterview. There appeared to be three or four tables in use even at this hour. She'd ask if they prepared food to go.

She hesitated at the register, but no waitress seemed available. A voice floated from the kitchen pass-through. "Take any seat. Menu's on the wall."

Not long on atmosphere, but the smell of bacon and eggs made Val weak. "I just wanted something to go. Do you do that?"

"We can try."

Val made eye contact with the cook. She blinked, not expecting her gaydar to zing at this hour of the morning. Mendocino seemed to be full of lesbians. "Shall I just tell you what I want?"

The cook blinked back, then said, "Sure."

Val crossed the dining room so she could study the menu. Her professional eyes crossed at the mishmash of decorating styles — old wallpaper and carpet clashed painfully with pedestal black lacquer tables with chairs that looked decidedly uncomfortable. She peeked into the kitchen as she went by, a habit her father had taught her. It seemed clean enough, but antiquated.

The menu was basic, but there were some surprising touches — roasted red peppers and feta cheese omelet for instance. A spinach and sweet onion soufflé sounded good, too. And what was Breakfast Pie?

A large moving van pulled up outside while she dithered, and a burly man pushed through the doors, heading straight for the kitchen with an air of grim finality.

"Where's Bill," Val heard him demand.

"I'm the new owner," the cook answered.

"Well, I have to take the tables and chairs. He hasn't made the payment in three months and the contract says I can take them after that. The three months are up today."

There was a stunned silence, then the cook said, "You mean they weren't paid for?"

Ouch. The travails of running a small business, especially a new one, Val thought. The two talked for a few more minutes, in lower tones, then the cook was seating the man at one of the tables, returning shortly with a cup of coffee and a slice of pie. As she did, one of the foursomes, all women, got up to leave.

"We left it on the table, Jamie dear. Delicious. Your aunt would have been so proud."

"Thanks, Monica. But don't go broke eating out on my account."

"Hard to do that here!" Monica and her group left with cheerful waves. Monica was right about the prices, too. Not as cheap as Denny's, by any means, but the food was a sight more palatable.

"Look, Ed," Jamie was saying. "Have a slice of Breakfast Pie and when I've caught up on my orders we can talk more."

Ed grunted and eyed the luscious-looking, but short pie. "Why's this Breakfast Pie?"

"Less sugar, more cinnamon and softer apples than regular pie. It's more like a German strudel on a good old American pie crust."

Ed grunted again, but from the rapt attention he paid to the pie after the first bite, Val guessed it was tasty.

"Now, what can I get you?"

Oh, Jamie was talking to her. Not an easy Sunday morning, waiting your own tables and doing the cooking, too.

"Um, I'd like two of the spinach soufflés —"

"They take about thirty minutes, if you can wait. Most folks call ahead. I keep meaning to write that on the menu board." Jamie tucked a wisp of hair the color of wheat back under her hair net.

"Oh. Well, I have about a ten-minute drive. What would travel well?"

Jamie frowned slightly, then said, "A fritatta, I think. Cross between an omelet and a quiche. It'll stay hotter, and be less fragile, cooks a heck of a lot faster than a soufflé. I can bake it in a disposable tin, too. Same price as an omelet."

Fritatta, schlmatta, whatever. Hey, she could work a fritatta into a column. Travels well, stays hot. Baked eggs. Interesting. "Sounds good. How about a largish fritatta with the peppers and feta cheese? Enough for two."

Jamie's eyes flicked, digesting that information. "How about some spinach or tomato, too?"

"No tomato. Gives her hives." Val saw Jamie digest the gender message as well. She wore her emotions close to the surface.

"Spinach then. Takes about fifteen minutes. You want hash browns or twice-fried potatoes with it?"

"Sounds good. The twice-fried thing." How did you twice fry potatoes? "And two slices of Breakfast Pie."

"Have a seat. Would you like some coffee while you wait? On the house," Jamie added, with something like a genuine smile. Yes, Val's gaydar was definitely zinging.

The coffee was heavenly. Rich and deep, cut with just a touch of fresh cream. Jamie bustled in the kitchen for a few minutes and a few more customers left, leaving money on the table and waving good-bye — what a trusting place. Jamie emerged a few minutes later to join Ed at his table.

"How'd you like the pie?"

Ed was actually smiling. What did she put in it, Prozac?

"Well, I'd say you have a fair chance of making a go of this place."

"I learned how from my aunt. She ran this place for over thirty years. I just bought it back. Bill was an idiot."

"You're telling me. I offered him some nice pine tables for rent, but he insisted on these fancy things."

"Do you have any idea what he did with the ones that were here?"

"Sold them to me. Said he needed cash and could make a rental payment. Bad deal all around, I think."

"Do you still have the tables?"

"Sorry, I don't. I found a good buyer over in Willits. But I've got something similar. Give you a good price for them. Not on rental, though, sorry."

Jamie sighed. "I'm afraid with the renovations I have to make to the kitchen — not to mention fixing the mess he made upstairs to the rooms. Well, there's not going to be much left."

They discussed the tables some more and Val's attention wandered. She was brought back to earth by the sharp ding of a timer. Jamie went back to the kitchen and returned shortly with two foil-wrapped dishes in a shallow cardboard box. She poured out two more cups of coffee into large covered Styrofoam cups and presented Val with a bill for a bit less than twenty dollars. Amazing, Val thought. It smelled delicious. She left a twenty and some singles on the counter — this woman needed every dollar she could get, apparently.

"I forgot your pie," Jamie called. "Hang on a second."

The door opened and Val heard the faint ringing of a church bell. All the patrons had departed for spiritual pursuits, perhaps. The man who came in had a clipboard. Uh-oh. Val knew what an inspector looked like. She'd seen enough inspectors to last her a lifetime.

Jamie added another foil-wrapped package to the

carton. "That's everything, I think." She turned inquiringly to the newcomer.

"Are you Ms. Onassis? I'm Ron Fortrell, county health department. I apologize for dropping in on a Sunday like this, but I'm going on vacation starting tomorrow and I thought why not get it out of the way."

"Makes sense," Jamie said. She hadn't even flinched. She must be ready, Val thought.

"By way of starting off I was wondering what progress you'd made on the list the previous owner had."

This time she flinched. "What list?"

"Well, for starters, he didn't pull a permit on that renovation work upstairs. I can't issue you an occupancy certificate until the work's been opened up for inspection."

"I can understand that," Jamie said, after a hard swallow. She led Ron — why were all inspectors named Ron? — into the kitchen. "But please tell me there was nothing significant in the kitchen."

"There was, but I see you've taken care of some of it already. The range hood —"

"Was disgusting and half clogged. As were the oven dampers. The fire extinguishers were expired."

"You've done good so far. Now about the doorway to the dining room. It's not A.D.A."

Shit, Val felt sorry for Jamie. When commercial property changed hands an inspector could arbitrarily decide that the premises needed to be brought into compliance with the Americans with Disabilities Act. The goal of the act was okay with Val, but the hit-and-miss application had put a spanner into more than one of Val's projects. And interpretation of the code varied from inspector to inspector. This was an old building. The doorway looked maybe two inches too narrow to Val.

"I'm real sorry about it," Ron was saying. "The previous owner was, well, he wasn't cooperative. Not in the least proactive. Wouldn't do anything unless I wrote it up, which made more work for me, and I had to keep coming out to check for clearances. So I wrote up the doorway and the back staircase. Sorry I can't do anything about it now. Your wheelchair lift is okay. But you have to have more space between these counters over here." Ron droned on about the heating and Val decided she'd eavesdropped long enough on *As the Stomach Turns*.

Jan was properly appreciative of the delicious breakfast. Val was amazed that fifteen minutes had resulted in something so delectable and light. Fritatta equaled major yums. The Breakfast Pie was the pièce de résistance. Delicious. She wondered if there was a Lunch Pie.


By lunchtime Jamie felt bludgeoned. The close of her first business week was definitely in the black, barely. Now she had to buy tables and chairs, or find a place that would rent them to her, and she had to contemplate major renovations to the kitchen because Bill had been an asshole to an inspector. She knew perfectly well that her bank balance would be close to zero when she paid for the new cooking equipment, stove and refrigerant unit for the walk-in she'd

ordered. She'd had more expense than she'd anticipated in laying in inventory — Bill had left the larder
bare. Not even salt left.

She'd also found out that Darlene hadn't had a
raise in three years and that the property taxes from
July to December were due in a few weeks, just after
Thanksgiving. Liesel had offered to lend her some
money, but she could only afford a few thousand. In
light of the new expenses, it wasn't enough to make a
difference. She *had* been a fool not get inspections
done.

She would need a bank loan for some working
capital. But where she'd find the cash flow to pay the
interest was another thing. Maybe in a few more
weeks she'd have a little more margin, but that was
doubtful. The townsfolk had all made an effort to
support her because of her relationship to Aunt Emily,
and so far everyone had been positive. It remained to
be seen if they'd keep coming back enough times to
make the difference. And if she could get some good
word-of-mouth to bring folks down from Fort Bragg.
Tourist season was a long way off.

Thank God for Dar, though. She was back to her
old self, gabbing and selling slices of pie to already
stuffed people, and she'd just popped in to suggest
that Jamie do Thanksgiving meals, pies and/or special
dishes for folks by pre-order, just as her aunt had.
Apparently a couple of people had asked if she'd be
returning to that tradition.

She took a moment at the rinse sink to close her
eyes, wondering when she'd be able to afford a
kitchen helper and closing on Mondays. She tried
sending her mind to the sandy, warm beaches of
Puerto Rico. Juan said it worked for him, but Jamie

wasn't as successful. Probably help more if she'd ever been there.

"I didn't think you'd have the nerve to come back."

A hot needle of pain shot through Jamie's back and for a moment she couldn't breathe. Serenity, she prayed. *If I can get past this, I can get past anything.*

She turned slowly, and said, "Nice to see you, too, Kathy."

Kathy had beautiful eyes. Jamie hadn't forgotten how the light blue contrasted so perfectly with her reddish-gold hair. Once upon a time she'd buried her face in that hair, felt its silkiness against her stomach.

It sparkled today with anger. "I can't believe you bought this dump."

Jamie couldn't stop her appalled gasp. "This was your home!"

"By all rights it should be mine right now, not yours." Kathy's mouth was more pinched than Jamie remembered. Still, she had lovely features. She could see what a man might want physically, though not what anyone could survive emotionally.

"I hear you're getting married."

"What's it to you? You'll never get married. You're as . . . as sick as she was and you don't have half her looks."

"Your mother was not sick." But you are, Jamie suddenly thought. Sick with dissatisfaction and unfulfilled dreams. A prom queen who had taken far longer than she had hoped to marry and settle down in the style she thought was owed her.

"She was a coward," Kathy snapped.

"What are you talking about?"

Kathy's pencil-thin eyebrows rose. "Didn't Liesel

81

tell you? She cut her wrists. All very neat and tidy in the bathtub."

Jamie's eyes unfocused. Aunt Emily had never been afraid of pain. She'd borne arthritis in her hips with hardly a murmur. What must she have been going through to kill herself? Was that why she hadn't wanted Jamie to know — afraid Jamie would ruin her resolve to end her suffering in her own way? She wished Liesel had told her the whole truth, but no doubt she had thought to protect Jamie's memory of her much-loved aunt. It was too much to take in.

"Is it any wonder I want to get out of this town? My mother committed suicide. She was a coward. She was a fucking dyke —"

Jamie gritted her teeth. "Watch your mouth. You're talking to a fucking dyke."

Kathy's upper lip curled. Jamie had a revelation — the ugliness of Kathy's nature showed on the outside. "So, you haven't changed your spots over the years."

"I suppose you think you have."

The sneer turned to ice. "Derek makes me very happy."

"I'm sure you think he does." Jamie wondered if Kathy was thinking about how they'd almost capsized the boat one afternoon. Surely she wasn't, so why couldn't Jamie stop thinking about it?

"And that's one more thing I have to say to you." Kathy stepped closer. "Just because you seduced me once —"

"More than once. And it was hardly one-way." Don't you remember, she wanted to add, how you hunted me down when I was berry-picking, how you couldn't seem to touch me enough?

82

"No — you seduced me. And no one is ever going to find out."

I should take out a full-page ad, Jamie thought. Was she finally past hoping Kathy would change? No . . . she wanted to hurt Kathy too much to be over it.

Val froze just outside the kitchen door when she heard the words "fucking dyke." It appeared her gaydar hadn't been at fault where the cook was concerned. This other woman was a piece of work, though. Good lord, this place was like a soap opera. She and Jan had decided to sample lunch here before heading home, but Val hadn't imagined that she'd eavesdrop on yet more diner drama. It wasn't as if she meant to — she was just on her way back from the bathroom.

"How exactly will you keep my mouth shut," the cook was saying.

There was a long silence during which Val knew she should stop listening, but of course she didn't.

Finally, the other woman said, "Isn't that a roach on the counter? And this milk is spoiled."

The cook said in a gasp, "You wouldn't dare."

"I'll make your life hell. Everyone knows this place is a disgrace. It'll never be what it was when Mother ran it." A bitter, hollow laugh. "This town ain't big enough for the both of us. Derek is the lawyer for all the big money interests in the county and —"

"How exactly will you explain your need to crush me to him?"

"It's enough that my mother left you her estate."

This was really juicy, Val thought, but enough was enough. She started to tiptoe away but the cook's next words were said with such pain that she froze.

"The difference between us is that I'd give every cent I have, and every cent I'll ever have, for her to be alive again — or even just to say good-bye."

"You may have lived in the same house with us, but you weren't her daughter."

"Neither were you. She never had all the happiness she could have had because you wouldn't let Liesel live with us."

"Who do you think you are? You're *nobody*. Your mother abandoned you. You don't even know who your father is. You're *nothing*. And this so-called inn of yours is *nothing*."

Val felt her spine stiffen. Energy surged up her arms. Nothing good ever came of these moments when she went with her feelings. It felt as if someone else was taking over her body. Her father called them moments of clarity. Val called them moments of madness.

She stepped into the doorway and said clearly, "The director from Viacom wants to know when they can start shooting the before pictures. They also want a projection of a finish date so they can bring some bigwig shareholders here for a party. Only if you do the cooking, of course. They especially want your crème brûlée." Creme brûlée was the only fancy dessert Val could name with any certainty that she was pronouncing it right.

The other woman was dressed in a tennis outfit that screamed "woman of leisure." Ugh. Her legs just weren't the type Val usually like to ogle in tennis skirts. Not at all the sort she preferred to drape over her shoulders. She was willing to bet that under those two-hundred-dollar cross-trainers the woman had bird feet to match the rest of her.

The cook looked stunned. If she didn't stop blinking she'd give the whole thing away.

"I thought you'd want to know," Val said. "Am I interrupting something?" She hooked her thumb into her belt loop and gave Birdy her best parted-lip smile. The one a friend had said could make Phyllis Schlafly think twice. "Haven't I seen you around?"

Birdy was flushing — anger or lust, who cared? Val turned the same smile on the cook but was met with a blank stare.

"Thanks for letting me know," the cook finally said. Geez, she'd never make a good liar. As if, Val's conscience reminded her, as if that was a bad thing.

"I'll be going," Birdy snapped, and then she flounced out the door with one last disdainful look at the premises.

"Was it something I said?" Val gave her full attention to the cook, who leaned heavily against the counter.

"You didn't have to do that."

"Yeah, so." Val shrugged. "I've never liked people who tortured small, defenseless creatures."

The flash from the cook's eyes seared Val in vivid green. She took a step backward.

"For your information," the cook said through stiff lips, "I am perfectly able to defend myself. I don't need your help. And who the hell are you anyway?"

Val assumed her usual bravado. "Valkyrie Valentine, at your service."

"Give me a break."

"I've got a birth certificate to prove it." Abruptly she got that sensation again — twice in one afternoon for a moment of madness was a record. Her head swirled with a desperate idea. Her mouth began operating before her brain engaged. "Can you cook? I mean really, really cook?"

"No, I can't. Not a bit. I run this place so I can mutilate vegetables with impunity."

Val wrinkled her nose. "I get it. Irony."

"Sarcasm. Irony is not knowing the difference."

"Forget I said anything."

"I will."

"Okay then."

"Fine."

They stared at each other. Val was thinking that Jamie must think her insane. Say something reasonable, she urged herself. Anything at all. "I need a cook." Not a great start, but it was something.

"I have a job." Jamie glanced meaningfully at the stove, then gasped. "Shit."

To Val's amazement, Jamie seized a frying pan and flipped the contents just by tweaking her wrist just so. She then carried a bubbling saucepan to a large blender and trickled the contents into a swirling mess of something red — it could be berries, Val guessed.

The waitress poked her head in. "Two more cacciatores. And I'm opening another bag of mixed greens. When you get a chance we could use another Thousand Island." She glanced curiously at Val but ducked out again.

Jamie left the blender running and came back to the stove. She flipped the contents of the pan again — wow, things could really be golden brown, Val realized — then said, "Did you have a point to make?"

"Yes." Val stepped closer and succeeded in making Jamie look her in the eyes, at least for a moment. "I need you and you need me." This is crazy, she told herself.

"How so?" Jamie reached into an overhead warmer for cooked chicken breasts.

"I need a cook. You need a builder."

"You're a builder." Jamie stopped slicing the chicken long enough to look Val up and down.

"Don't judge a book by its cover. I can widen that doorway." She stepped back to glance at the hallway. Messy, but doable. Not cheap, though. Carpet had to go. It would look good with skylighting, too. "And the stairwell. I can rebuild this place from the ground up. In fact, I need to. In a pretty short time frame."

"Do you always listen to other people's conversations?"

"Yes. It's what I live for."

"And what would you get out of this arrangement?"

"I get to show the place off. I get someone to do the cooking behind the scenes while I show it off. I become famous. You get your renovations. Everybody's happy."

"You're nuts."

"Yes. Oh, and you'll need to make shrimp scampi at least once. I have a good recipe."

"So do I. But no one said I was agreeing to anything."

"Are you willing to talk?"

"Only if you have a psychiatrist's note."

"And here I was thinking you didn't have a sense of humor."

"And here I was thinking you didn't have your

wits. Look, I'm busy." Jamie ladled a pungent red sauce, thick with enormous sliced mushrooms and artichoke hearts, onto the sliced chicken breasts, which had been fanned out across the plate. She added a ring of raw red onion to each, then set them up under lamps on the pass-through.

"Mind if I look around?"

"Be my guest."

Val did a quick tour of the botched mess upstairs, then made her way back to Jan. "Sorry I was gone so long."

Jan pointed at the menu. "I'm thinking of having the spaghetti carbonara if it doesn't have tomatoes. I think we're here on Italian day."

"Cacciatore for me. And I need a big favor. Well, I need some understanding."

"Don't we all?"

"I need to stay here for a few hours. Maybe overnight. I have an idea, a big, fabulous idea about renovating this place, but I haven't convinced the owner."

"I have to be in Pacifica first thing in the morning," Jan said. "And if we wait here much longer we'll be bumper-to-bumper getting through Napa."

"Well, maybe I can take a bus home tomorrow."

"You're nuts." Jan was definitely a little miffed, but she had a little bit of quirk to her lips.

"So I've been told." Val glanced at the ceiling joists. Hmm. "I really need to see if I can work this out. I'll tell you all about it when I hire you to do the fine work."

"Then I'd be sleeping with the boss. I've never done that before," Jan said. To Val's relief, she was smiling.

"Forgive me for ducking out on the end of our weekend?"

"Yes, on one condition."

"Name it."

"That we have dinner and breakfast at my place this Friday."

Val grinned. "I can live with that. It's a sacrifice, but I can do it."

Jan threw a packet of Sweet 'n' Low at her. "You *are* nuts."

Jan didn't know the half of it.

# Broccoli Salad

I am not a big broccoli fan, but this salad changed my mind! It's easy enough for almost anyone to make and keeps well for up to 3 days.

4 cups (2 heads) bite-size broccoli florets and stems
1/2 sweet red onion, sliced into rings
with large rings cut into quarters
1 cup raisins (regular and/or golden raisins okay)
1 cup celery, sliced
1/2 cup coarsely chopped walnuts or pecans
1/2 cup coarsely chopped water chestnuts (optional)
1/4 cup rice wine vinegar
1/4 cup light vegetable oil
1/4 cup sugar
1/2-2/3 cup mayonnaise

PREPARATION:

Plump the raisins by covering them with hot water for 5 minutes. Drain well. Combine all vegetables and nuts in a salad bowl large enough to allow for tossing and that has a good sealing lid. If you're picky about such things, feel free to blanch the broccoli; I don't think it's necessary. Use some of the broccoli stems, but only what is immediately adjacent to the florets. Farther down the stems are too stringy to enjoy eating raw.

METHOD:

In a small bowl combine the rice wine vinegar, oil, sugar and mayonnaise and beat thoroughly until well blended. Pour over broccoli mix and toss. Place in refrigerator for at least 4 hours before serving; overnight is even better. Occasionally stir settled dressing back through salad, or turn over and shake if the lid is tight enough. Serves 6 or so and is easy to double for a party.

 *From the Waterview, Mendocino*

# 6

"I don't see why we have to lie. I'm very uncomfortable even thinking about it."

Val sighed. This woman was way too straight for a dyke. "Let me explain it one more time." Each time she explained it, Val got more terse. Jamie made it sound so . . . illicit. "I need to prove to this magazine chain that I can garden, renovate, decorate and cook. With me so far?"

Jamie pursed her lips. "You need to use words with fewer syllables."

"Now I recognize the sarcasm." Val could purse

her lips, too. "I don't know why this is so difficult to conceptualize."

"Because you can't cook. It's like lying on a job application."

"Let me worry about my own personal brimstone."

Jamie's eyes said she was certain Val had a lot to worry about in that department. "You think you can just pretend to cook? No one will ask you how a dish was prepared? You think you can talk the talk without breaking a few eggs?"

"What a beautifully mixed metaphor," Val said sweetly. She was starting to have second thoughts. "How hard can it be?"

Jamie glowered. "If it's so easy, why can't you do it?"

"I don't know about *can't*, I've just never applied myself to it."

"Then all you need is a crash course in cooking from somebody. I'm busy."

"I also need a place I've worked on myself."

"How many lies have you told?"

"They're not lies. Just a little literary license. Do you know how many travel articles are written by people who never leave home?"

"Do you know how many cookbooks are written by people who don't test the recipes themselves? I hate that."

"Oh, so literary license is taken in the cooking industry, too?"

"And if everyone jumped off a cliff—"

"How old *are* you?" Major regrets. She had not expected Jamie to be so . . . so . . . stodgy.

Jamie's eyes flashed. "I have a dream. It's not a

big dream. It's just a little dream. But it's my dream. Someday I'll write a cookbook. And it will be authentic. I'll test all the recipes myself. It will be easy to follow and it will be an underground success. Like *The Enchanted Broccoli Forest*."

"Broccoli? Enchanted? What does that have to do with you cooking while I renovate? I just mean a temporary thing!"

"We'll be found out," Jamie said stonily. "It would be mortifying."

"You think that getting your renovations done by a professional for free is not worth the risk of some embarrassment?"

"One-hundred-percent free?"

"Well, my time would be free."

"How good are you?"

Val's smile turned smug. "As good as your Breakfast Pie." She was pleased to see a hint of a smile touch Jamie's expression.

"This is insane."

"I'd be done, say, by New Year's. If I gave it my all and then some." She would find ways to put Sheila off until then. She'd invite Sheila for shrimp scampi on New Year's Eve. They'd dine in style, tour Val's masterpiece renovation, enjoy crème brûlée in front of the fire — she'd install a fireplace if she had to — and the rest would be entertainment history. This would be easy.

Jamie was shaking her head. "I'm insane to even be listening to you. And I should be making salad dressing for dinner and caramelizing onions." She rose as if to end the discussion.

"Won't you at least sleep on it? I gave up a car

ride home to talk to you." Val batted her eyelashes ever so slightly. Sometimes it worked, even on the most stodgy of personalities.

Jamie had been going to say no, Val could see it in her eyes. But instead she shrugged and said, "Whatever."



"This woman is for real?" Liesel poured out a steaming mug of hot chocolate.

Jamie dropped contentedly into the welcoming easy chair and accepted the mug. "I don't know. She claims she writes a column for *Sunrise*. But she also admits that she makes stuff up about cooking. So how do I know if she makes up stuff about construction and renovations?"

Liesel was rummaging through a basket full of magazines. "I bought a copy of it not too long ago. It should be in . . . here it is." She thumbed to the table of contents. "Well, I'll be. 'Wall Glazing,' by Valkyrie Valentine."

Jamie took the magazine. There was no photo but it did tend to suggest that this woman was not a complete lunatic. Maybe, with a little practice, she wouldn't be a total loss at cooking. It seemed to Jamie that glazing a wall took almost as much patience and skill as icing a cake or forming pastilles. "Well, maybe she's not an idiot."

"I'd be happy to talk to her, too, if you want me to."

Jamie sipped the wonderful chocolate, then smiled fondly at Liesel. "I'd love you to. And thank you for not saying I told you so about the repairs."

"Jacob will. But it's so right that you bought it back. Em would be very pleased to know that you did. Maybe you paid too much, maybe not. Does it matter?"

"I want the place to be livable again. It feels empty without people upstairs. And the boarders provide a steady income stream, too. It's a little less stressful buying eggs for the week if you know you've got a base of customers for breakfast. Remember Jill? She traded rent for working in the kitchen, too. I sure could use that."

"Everything will be fine, *liebchen*. Drink your chocolate and stop worrying. You're as bad as Em."

Jamie did as she was told, then devoured some savory biscuits that Liesel supplied, complete with paprika butter.

"These are yummy. Mind if I swipe the recipe?"

"I'd be honored. And now I'm going to bed."

"Night-night." Jamie knew she had to head for bed herself or she'd never hear her five-thirty alarm, but she was too wound up with possibilities to go to sleep right away. She eventually stretched out in the dark and envisioned The Waterview restored to working condition. If Valkyrie Valentine could do that without Jamie having to hock her soul, then so be it. What was a little deception along the way?

Jamie was leaning against the kitchen door when a thump at the service entrance brought her out of a snatched moment of relaxation. Valkyrie Valentine was clanking into her kitchen with a toolbox and a large level under one arm.

"What do you think you're doing?" Jamie planted herself between Val and an oven full of delicate puff pastry for one of Jacob's charters.

"Widening your door two inches or more. I borrowed the tools."

"You can't make a mess in here. Sawdust, and who knows what in the food —"

"There won't be much of a mess, just some ruined paint and wallpaper. Might get a few paint chips on the floor."

Jamie blinked in astonishment as Val planted the hook end of a hammer behind one of the doorjambs and pulled experimentally. "We haven't agreed to anything —"

"I'll do this with no strings attached. Fair warning, you'll need to paint and I can't guarantee that this jamb isn't going to split, so you might need to replace it too. Your door will be wider by more than two inches, too." Val ran a flat black thing over the wall next to the doorjamb. It looked like a remote control to Jamie. A couple of small lights lit up and Val grinned. "Thought so. Like most old houses the spacers are closer together near a door."

"But —"

"It'll be more like four and a half inches wider. I'll just use the next spacer for the jamb. Sometimes things work out easier because of the non-standard construction. Oh, and you can't paint or tidy this up until the inspector's okayed it. We'll probably need to pull a permit retroactively, but we can do it for the whole renovation for a single fee, then."

"I haven't agreed to —" The rest of Jamie's sentence was drowned out in the groaning shriek of the doorjamb splitting away from the wall. Nails screamed as Val's hammer relentlessly pried them from their beds.

Keeping wide-eyed track of Val's progress, Jamie kneaded bread dough, chopped broccoli for salad, made a new batch of blue cheese dressing and stirred together a simple syrup for berry topping while Val systematically separated the doorjamb from the wall and then sawed away the wallboard. To Jamie's amazement, the wallboard peeled back a little more than four inches to reveal another wall stud.

Val snorted. "Good news, this is all dry. I don't see any creepy crawlies, either."

"That's good," Jamie said. She tried to sound knowledgeable. She peered out into the dining room, but there were still only a few people, all locals. They'd forgive the noise.

Val was examining the wood she'd pulled off. "One of these is worthless, but I can use the other. You want me to put it on the dining room side of the door — it'll look better than nothing."

"Please," Jamie said. She poured the simple syrup into whirling olallieberry puree and left the blender to run for a few minutes while the syrup cooled. She pulled three beautiful double-sized pound cakes out of the upper oven.

"That smells wonderful," Val said.

"Winter shortcake," Jamie explained. "Pound cake and berry syrup smothered in whipped cream with macerated berries on top." She wiped her hands and scootched around Val to add the dessert to the menu board under "Today only."

Dar looked up from her magazine. "Bill used to carp at me for taking a load off when there were only a few tables busy. Didn't matter to him that I'd filled the sugars, topped off the ketchup, checked the napkins and wiped down the chairs for good measure."

"Bill was a horse's ass," Jamie said with more than a little heat. It was the morning lull — the few customers there were quite happy, so why shouldn't Dar have a rest?

"He didn't tell you a bunch of stuff, huh? Well, seems like this Val woman is a godsend, then. I loaned her Harry's old tools, I hope that's okay. She's gonna have that door done before the lunch crowd."

Jamie glanced over her shoulder. The work was progressing rapidly, but she still gave Val a narrow glance. Chatting up Dar, was she? That was sneaky.

Val caught Jamie's glance and wondered what she'd done wrong. She'd have asked if her mouth hadn't been full of nails. It had been a while since she'd driven this many nails by hand, and so quickly. She'd set a mental goal for the project of an hour and she wanted to meet it. She wanted Ms. Stodgy Snotty Jamie to be impressed, goddammit. She wanted to get her hands on this inn and bring Sheila Thintowski out here to see it.

Dar had proved to be a goldmine of information. She'd learned that Jamie Onassis had just bought her aunt's inn back from a loser, that the aunt was a saint and a terrific cook and had just died, that Jamie wasn't really her niece, that the aunt was a lesbian, that Jamie had had a romantic setback early in life and was probably still not over it. Val had enough intuition to know that Birdy from yesterday was the source of the romantic setback. What Jamie might have ever seen in her was beyond Val's comprehension. It didn't bode well for Jamie's sense.

Dar wouldn't say anything negative about anybody, though, even when Val had led her in that direction. She had gone so far as to say that Birdy — Kathy — was the aunt's daughter and that the two hadn't gotten along. Small wonder. But today as she worked Val had a little sense of the halo Emily Smitt had left on this place. If enough grime was scrubbed off, it would shine again. Jamie clearly had the talent for that.

She swallowed a curse as a splinter bit its way past her heavy gloves. She put her back into the last few nails, then ran the level up the jamb. Nice. The lintel needed replacing, too, because it had to be a solid piece, but that would be easy enough to pick up at a lumber yard. She'd have to find out if Jamie had any preferences in moulding or if she'd want the flat, wide Shaker look that adorned some, but not all, of the doors. Hmm. Shaker. Simple lines, inexpensive and elegant. That wouldn't be bad as a guiding theme.

She swept the dining room with her gaze and visualized scrubbed tables and cushioned benches, the central overhead lights in heavy glass with hidden tracks for the rest. Walls glazed with whitewash and blue Shaker patterns. It would be lovely. Add some Shaker rugs on the walls, more utilitarian but compatible runners between the tables, knock out that side wall for an energy-efficient gas fireplace, and it would look like a million bucks. And it would suit Jamie's food.

Speaking of which, Val was going to lose her mind from the scent of something bubbling on the stove. When she thought Jamie wasn't looking she nipped over and took a deep breath. Ohmigosh — clam chowder. Fresh clam chowder with bacon and chives.

Small rounds of French bread stood next to the stove — edible bowls? She swiped a curl of a hard grated cheese. Tangy. Cheese on clam chowder? Yes, that cheese would be good. Wow. She could eat the entire pot.

"Want some?"

Cheezit, the cops. "Sure," Val said, holding back a blush. "Remember when I said my time was free? I lied."

"No!"

Val wanted to smack Jamie. But she smiled instead. "Almost free. You have to feed me, and my appetite is not dainty."

A ghost of a smile passed over Jamie's lips. Val realized she hadn't seen a real smile yet. "It'll be my pleasure."

Val watched with anticipatory pleasure as Jamie scooped out a round loaf and filled it with chowder, sprinkled cheese on the top and put the whole thing under the broiler. Yum. She frowned when Jamie added a small bowl of broccoli salad to the serving plate. Well, heck, she'd give it a try.

"I'll just clean up," Val said. "Um, we have a deal then?"

Jamie took a deep breath. "We have a deal." She glanced around as if she expected lightning and thunder.


I flew back to New York in the middle of November, just a few days before Thanksgiving. I had a pile of projections and demographics, results of a focus group and the Valentine tape. I'd made a business appointment with my father through his assistant and asked that Graham Chester, *Sunrise*'s executive editor, attend as well.

As I walked to his office I felt a thrill of apprehension. I was unused to proving myself to my father, at least not so directly. This project was my baby from start to finish and I didn't want to disappoint him in front of Graham. I wondered if I should have asked to see Daddy alone. No, I didn't want Daddy selling this to everyone else who needed to come on board. No one would take it, or me, seriously if I didn't carry the ball, curry cooperation and generate enthusiasm all by myself.

Graham kissed me on both cheeks when I entered. He was as queer as a three-dollar bill, to use an old expression, and loved to flirt with women. When I saw *Victor/Victoria* I thought the role of Toddy had been based on Graham. He'd been my father's close friend for many, many years. That he was homosexual didn't bother my father at all. That was probably why he had never questioned my sexuality, just questioned me on the quality of who was sharing my bed and, occasionally, my life.

Graham held me at arm's length and raised an eyebrow. "Chanel again? Are you trying to impress little old me?"

"You're easy." I nodded in Daddy's direction. "It's him I'm trying to impress."

"Sheila, you've always impressed me," Daddy said.

"As a daughter. Today I hope to change that." I set down my portfolio. "I hope to show you how an investment in a woman named Valkyrie Valentine can grow into a merchandising and franchise opportunity that will put Warnell Communications at the top of the heap."

Both men still had mildly indulgent expressions, but I didn't break form. I handed them both a bound booklet and a two-page executive summary. I ticked off the items quickly — they could both read.

"An unknown personality. Focus group results project wide demographics starting at age twenty-six for women and thirty-six for men. Name is memorable and real. Father is career military, mother a legal secretary. Competition in the cable market is strong, but Valentine offers complete home, garden and kitchen know-how. Background check clean. She is an open lesbian, but her initial audiences are going to be large cities where that won't raise any boycotts. As for appearance . . ."

I handed them stills from the video that showed Val in her jeans and workshirt. It made my palms damp.

Graham whistled. "If she makes *my* heart go pitty-pat imagine what she'll do to everyone else."

Daddy was staring at her picture with a faint smile. "She's got something, I'll say that."

"Part of her something was turned up by the back-ground check. She had cosmetic surgery on her nose recently." I handed over a photo from her high school yearbook. "I don't think anyone will hold that against her."

Graham chortled. "My God, no, I don't think so. She makes Cyrano look like a pug."

I went on with my summary, then directed them to the bound report I'd given them. In it were projections that I'd developed with the marketing staff in Dallas. Marguerite Dennison, who had accurately predicted *Tomorrow's Gourmet*'s niche sales, had helped. I knew Daddy would be reassured by Marguerite's name on the numbers.

"I've given some thought to our choices of cable networks," I went on. "We could probably put Valentine anywhere. Discovery, Home and Garden, The Learning Channel. I think we make them bid for it. We can offer all the publicity in the world for them. And I think we'd be very smart to offer a six-episode mini-marathon to public television stations for their pledge breaks, and at a very reasonable cost. Builds goodwill and a lot of people will think Valentine is already famous someplace else and only now coming to their town."

"You're devious," Graham said. "I like it."

"We have a viable product to offer."

"This Valentine woman — she's on board?" Daddy glanced at her picture again.

"Yes, I think so. I haven't discussed contract points with her, but she's . . . hungry."

Graham said, "I'll ask her editor what makes her tick. Her column work has always been competent, and she's been flexible about content. Until her more recent columns, I didn't know she could cook. I've never met the woman, actually."

"Sheila, this really is excellent work," Daddy said.

"I hear a 'but.' "

"But. It's a lot to hang on one person. I want to be sure, absolutely sure, that she's on board. That she can sustain something of this scope."

"I understand that," I said, wondering what he had in mind.

"I'd like to meet her myself. I've been thinking

about that article you gave me to read. I also read a few more. We're not going to be selling her recipes, or her looks, or how wonderfully she can wallpaper the Sistine Chapel. We're selling an entire package — that's the marketing edge you've identified. We're selling the Complete Woman. Better than a mom, better than a wife, better than a sister. If she's not all that, then we could lose our shirts."

"I don't think meeting her is a problem. In fact, I think it's essential."

"I don't just want to meet her," Daddy said. He had a nostalgic look on his face that puzzled me. "I want to experience the Complete Woman. Experience her hospitality, taste her food, see and touch her creativity. If it's real to me, we can make it real to America."

"When would you like to do this?" I had no idea if Val could entertain my father and his entourage. Her home sounded large from her writing, but I didn't know how large. I could help her work it out. Stick the assistants in a motel. With Christmas coming up most of them would beg off, anyway.

"I've been thinking about the holidays. With Marissa out of the picture —"

"I didn't know that." Good-bye, Marissa of the helpless fingernails.

"A new development."

It explained the nostalgic look. He wanted to experience home life, the Way Things Ought To Be — at least to his way of thinking. "You mean Christmas?"

"She's always writing about doing some large entertaining at Christmas, so it shouldn't be too much of an imposition. We'd be just a few more bodies. It would make up my mind. A chance to get to know each other better."

Christmas on the Coast. He wanted the whole roaring fire, egg nog, singing carols, mistletoe and holly, and twinkling lights event. *Merde.* I didn't know if Val could cope. Surely she had plans already.

Graham gestured with Val's picture. "This makes me want to come along for the ride."

"Do that," Daddy urged.

"Are you crazy?" Graham rolled his eyes. "My calendar is already crammed with parties. I have no intention of missing my favorite shoulder-rubbing time of the year. San Francisco is a tempting idea, I will admit, but I'm not budging."

"I might make you change your mind . . . just for a few days."

Graham sighed. "You'll have to do better than that." He glanced at me. "It had better be worth it."

"It will be," I promised.

I had no idea what I'd just committed myself to. All I knew was that I was right about turning Valkyrie Valentine into a gold mine, and I'd do just about anything to make it happen. And I sure as hell wanted to see her again, and convince her that I could offer her a partnership that would be mutually satisfying. I could make her dreams come true. I had realized that I'd been waiting all my life for this opportunity, and this woman. There was no time to lose.

# Simple Cheese Soufflé

| WHITE SAUCE (ROUX) | EGGS & CHEESE |
|---|---|
| 1 cup milk, any kind | 6 eggs, separated (see below) |
| 1/2 stick unsalted butter | 3/4 to 1 cup coarsely grated very |
| or margarine | sharp cheddar (3 year or older) |
| 4-6 Tbsp flour | 1/2 tsp cayenne pepper |

## PREPARATION:

Coat a baking dish (soufflé pan or 3qt baker) with butter or non-stick cooking spray. Pat sides with grated Parmesan if desired (not the canned kind). Separate eggs, putting the whites into a tall mixing bowl. Beat yolks together.

## WHITE SAUCE:

Heat milk in medium (2-3qt) saucepan slowly, on medium, but don't scald. A larger saucepan makes later steps easier, but beware that the larger bottom might heat faster and scald or burn the mix. Add butter, stir until melted. Add flour one tablespoon at a time, stirring briskly with a whisk to eliminate lumps. If mixture becomes clumpy, add more milk, one tablespoon at a time. Mixture should begin to thicken but still be runny.

## EGGS & CHEESE:

Add cheese to still slightly runny white sauce and stir until all cheese is melted. Remove from heat. Stir in egg yolks and cayenne. While mixture cools, beat egg whites until soft peaks form. Mixer is easiest, though with a copper bowl you can do it with a hand whisk.

Add 1/4 of egg whites to the cooled cheese mixture, stirring thoroughly. Beat remaining egg whites again if they drooped. Gently fold remaining egg whites into the cheese mixture and pour into baking dish. Wipe away any mixture on the lip of the baking dish then run a spatula about 1/4-inch around the inside of the rim. Bake 50-60 minutes. Soufflé is done when knife inserted into center has no clear liquid on it. If the top gets very brown before it is done, turn down the heat 50° and add 15 minutes to cooking time .

## Tip

Why unsalted butter? Creameries usually use higher quality cream with better taste since salt won't be added. You can always add salt later.

❖❖❖❖❖❖❖❖ *From the Waterview, Mendocino* ❖❖❖❖❖❖❖❖

# 7

In the end Val made it back to San Francisco on Wednesday, courtesy of Jamie's friend, Liesel Hammond. Val didn't know if the older woman really had the burning need to drive to San Francisco that week or whether she was hoping to check out Val's credentials during the long car ride.

As it turned out, she need not have been so suspicious. Liesel was bound for a retirement dinner for an old friend from her Army days. Val appreciatively eyed the neatly pressed and pristine dress uniform hanging in the back seat.

"Pardon me for asking, but did you emigrate to the U.S. and then join the Army?"

"Oh no, I was born here. I just didn't learn English until I went to school. Around five or so. I've never lost the accent."

"What was it like, being gay in the military?"

"I wasn't really gay then. At least, I wasn't sure. I had nothing to tell about." Liesel kept both hands on the wheel as she drove, something Val appreciated after the hellish ride up with Jan.

"Oh, that explains it. Sorry I'm so nosy."

"If you don't ask, how will you know?"

Val agreed. "Very true. So what do you think about Don't Ask, Don't Tell?"

"It assumes that no one talks about their private life on duty when in truth that's all there is to talk about sometimes. I think they dreamed it up because no one wants to confront the real truth."

"That the military is homophobic?"

Liesel shook her head. "No, that many men in the military are sexual predators. They assume that all men are like them, so when they think of a gay man in the shower with them — well, what they're really thinking is how terrible it would be if that gay man were to do to them what they do to women. They get hysterical over the idea that a gay man might sexually harass them because they do it themselves and get away with it. When the issue becomes about appropriate conduct then it won't matter who is what. That's the way it ought to be. Not this shameful silence."

"Yes, ma'am," Val said. "You are correct, ma'am."

Liesel laughed. She had a nice, hearty laugh that

underscored her faint accent. "Were you a military brat?"

"Yes, ma'am. Brat, ma'am." Val grinned. "My father will die in the saddle. My parents divorced when I was seven, and my dad had custody of me. My mom wasn't interested." She realized that a little of that old hurt was still there. She hadn't thought about it in ages. "Anyway, living with Dad meant exotic locations, like, oh, Kansas. Actually, it was great because on-base facilities were decent for kids. Always a swimming pool, sometimes a library. And always the machine shop or motor pool for the lieutenant's tomboy daughter to hang around in. I always knew I wanted to make things, make something out of nothing with my own hands. My dad didn't care about what I decided to do for a living as long as I went to college first."

"How does your father feel about your career now?"

"Oh, he tends to think my columns are just reports after scrimmage. In a way they are — writing about projects is not as fun as doing them. But it's still fun enough to make me feel slightly guilty about making money doing something I like so much." Val realized that something about Liesel made her want to laugh — the exact opposite of how serious Jamie made her feel.

Liesel said something really foul-sounding in German as a slow-moving van failed to use a turnout. "We can't pass for another seven, eight miles now. Oh well. Your father sounds like he did an okay job."

"I have no complaints, not at this late date," Val said. "It took me a few years to adjust. But when you're thirty-four you either give up being pissed about stuff they couldn't control anyway or you stay mad for the rest of your life. My dad tried hard to do right by me."

"Any feelings about being a parent yourself?"

"Lord — I haven't thought about it at all. Do you have any kids?"

"No, not unless you count Jamie. I've known her since she was nine, when I started dating Em. Twenty years. She was always such a serious child. Probably because her mother was such a flake. Left the child with Em and never came back for her. Can you imagine?"

Val couldn't. "Emily sounds like a wonderful person."

Liesel's hands tightened on the steering wheel. "She was. A heart like the Grand Canyon."

"I don't mean to pry — but how exactly did she die?"

"Somebody's been talking?"

"Not to me, to Jamie."

Liesel's knuckles went white. "They told her that Em committed suicide. Who? Dar wouldn't have said."

"Some woman named Kathy."

"That *bitch*." Liesel looked murderous. "I caught Jamie looking at me a couple of times these last few days, like she wanted to say something. Poor thing. I should have told her, but she adored Em. I was afraid she'd think Em had failed her somehow."

"She told Kathy off."

"Good. I have never in all my born days seen a creature with so little filial devotion. The more Em gave up for her, the more she wanted. Em took out a

110

second mortgage for Kathy's perfect smile, her nose, her ears, and I don't know what all."

"How big was her nose?" The question slipped out before Val thought better of it, but she was curious. "I had my nose done about seven months ago. Major sinus problems afterward."

Liesel gave Val a look that said she hadn't realized Val was vain enough to have her nose done. "It wasn't big, just a little crooked. It had charm, now it's just ordinary."

"My nose was like this." Val demonstrated. "The guys in the motor pool called me Durante. Heck, my dad did too. I was sort of proud of it, but — it was a honker. I'll be honest, if I didn't want to be on TV I wouldn't have touched it."

"What do you want to do on TV?"

Val told Liesel all about her plans, and then how Sheila Thintowski had materialized to make her dreams come true. "Didn't Jamie tell you about all of that?"

"She's so tired when she gets home that we only talk about immediate things. But she did say you're hoping to show the place off when you're done, to get a job."

"Well, I'm hoping to get more than a job. I'm hoping to make a name for myself. A national name, like Bob Villa, the *This Old House* guy."

"I thought Jamie was going to teach you how to cook."

"That's just to make an honest woman out of me. I've been writing about cooking a little in my columns, but it's all based on research, not doing. I couldn't fool anyone for long."

"Oh. Well, Jamie's got the patience to teach you, that's for sure. Thank heaven, we can pass this idiot at last."

Liesel zoomed around the van so competently that Val wished she could give Jan driving lessons. She wished that Liesel owned the inn, not Jamie. They'd have a blast working on it together.

When she got home, Val found her answering machine blinking frantically and a total of eleven messages from Sheila Thintowski. Sheila begged Val to call her immediately, in increasing levels of exasperation and agitation.

Val did time calculation and figured she could catch Sheila at the number in Texas — it was still business hours there.

"Where have you been?" Sheila wasted no time on pleasantries.

"Working on the inn," Val said, quite truthfully.

"You need to keep up on your messages," Sheila said. "Everything could fall apart here if you don't get your act together."

"Whoa," Val said. "Let's start over. What's the rush?" Sheila had no call to get so snippy.

"My — the head of Warnell Communications is coming to visit you."

"Mark Warnell? Visiting me?" Val fumbled for a chair and sat down in a heap. "When?"

"For Christmas. He is very intrigued by the idea of making you Warnell's Martha Stewart. But he has to be convinced you are — as he put it — the Complete Woman."

Val's head was spinning. Christmas was five weeks away. It was going to be a stretch getting most of the work done by New Year's — done enough to impress Sheila, at least. But Mark Warnell? By Christmas? Impossible. "Do I have any say in this?"

There was a silence on Sheila's end that said Sheila thought Val mad for even asking. "Are you interested in vaulting to national prominence or not?"

"Of course I am," Val said shakily. She was mad. This was insanity.

"Mark Warnell wants to experience Christmas on the Coast — like you wrote about in your column. He's actually a very sentimental man. It would be just me and him visiting. Possibly Graham Chester as well."

"Graham Chester," Val echoed weakly. She'd never even met *Sunrise*'s executive editor.

"So we're on, right? I'll call with details. If you'd like I can fly out sometime soon and develop an itinerary for the visit. I know Mr. Warnell's tastes fairly well. I've known him for many years."

"I don't think that will be necessary," Val said. Panic beat at her eardrums, making it hard to hear. "The place I'd like to entertain Mr. Warnell is actually not in San Francisco. I took a little literary license there. If my readers knew that I lived literally on the coast and in an old inn, they'd never think they could accomplish the projects I write about. That I was some lady of leisure with a staff of twelve — which is hardly the case. So I chose San Francisco as a base. I just have an apartment there."

"Where exactly is this inn?"

"Mendocino."

"Really?" Sheila sounded moderately pleased. "I've always heard that's a charming little place. Mr. Warnell will love it."

"That's great, then," Val said.

"Well, I'll let you know our schedule. Do you have a fax up there? And what's the phone number?"

Val gave Sheila the phone number for the inn and mentally added her fax machine to the list of things to bring up with her. Her Subaru was going to be loaded.

She wandered aimlessly around the apartment gathering things she was going to take, the enormity of Mark Warnell's visit not yet sinking in. By Christmas. She had to renovate the Waterview by Christmas. There was not a moment to spare. She already knew Jamie had a lot of extra cooking planned for Thanksgiving, and that was next week.

It could be done. No other option was available. She'd have to hire more people than she thought. Jamie's budget was really tight, so the extra people might end up being her investment.

Christ! She had until Christmas to learn to cook. Really cook. Mark Warnell was not going to be fooled by a single meal Jamie whipped up and Val served. Sheila and Mr. Warnell would be there for several days — egads! As many as twelve or thirteen entire *meals* They'd linger in the kitchen to chat while Val cooked.

What had she gotten herself into? It wasn't as if she'd been backed into a corner by a lie — well, okay, she had. But if she could only turn the lie to truth she would achieve her dreams.

Five weeks. It would be two weeks before she got

114

her permit to start work, and two weeks was a miracle by San Francisco standards. Things weren't quite so busy in Mendocino. Well, she would spend the next two weeks doing whatever could be done without a permit — painting and wallpapering. And cooking lessons.

This was madness.

She only went to bed because she knew that if she didn't sleep she'd never stay awake for the long drive back to Mendocino. She stared at the pattern the streetlights made seeping past the blinds. With Jamie's permission, she had moved into the most usable room on the second floor of the inn, and even without blinds the nights were dark, the mornings quiet. She found herself startling awake at the slightest noise and she wondered if country life would ruin her.

"You're folding the egg whites, not beating them into submission. Be gentle." Jamie was almost at the end of her rope. Val really wasn't a stupid person, but her lack of patience with cooking steps was wearing Jamie ragged.

"Why does it matter?"

"Your goal is to keep as much air as possible in the egg whites. No air equals a flat soufflé. If I wanted a flat soufflé I'd make an omelet."

Val stared down at the bowl as if it contained poison. "I don't get why it's called folding."

"I don't know why it's called folding," Jamie said. Honestly, Val was like a four-year-old. "Why is grout called grout?"

"It's from *grut*, an Old English —"

115

"Forget I asked," Jamie snapped. "You fold like this. Scoop down the side of the bowl, lift the mixture, then carry it to the other side of the bowl, lower it in, then back to the other side of the bowl to lift again. It's like . . . like folding towels."

"Right." Val looked confused, but she took the bowl back and copied Jamie's motions relatively well.

"That's right. Just go slow and be gentle. Think airy thoughts." Jamie sped back to processing nuts for vegetarian mincemeat. Thanksgiving was three days away — two, really, since it was late Monday evening — and no vacation for her. Dar's suggestion that she take orders for pies and meals had proven lucrative, but there were not enough hours in the day. She'd forgotten that Thanksgiving week always brought extra tourists, so dining room traffic was up. Then she had all the extra pies and meals to make for Thanksgiving itself. There just wasn't time to show Val the finer points of cooking.

The dining room was mostly empty by now, and Dar poked her head in. "I'm off, Jamie. Tips were good today. And folks really liked the cranberry cake."

"Dar, you're a jewel," Jamie said. "Thanks for working the extra hours. Can you make it back early in the morning?"

"Sure, but I can't Wednesday morning. And I'd like to get home Wednesday night reasonable like. Have my own turkey to make, you know. But my niece is visiting, and she'd jump to make some extra cash. Can I bring her by Tuesday for dinner rush? You remember her. Nancy? She'd only want minimum plus tips."

"Sure I do. That would be great. All this extra

work means I can pay for some extra help. You were working way too hard tonight, too."

"It's nice for a change," Dar said. But it was clear to Jamie that Dar was tired.

"You're lucky to have her," Val said after Dar had left.

"Don't I know it."

"I think these are mixed," Val said. "I thought about balloons and clouds all the time I stirred."

Jamie found herself smiling helplessly. She could be so annoyed with Val, then find herself responding to Val's undeniable charm. But she swore she wouldn't succumb to it. Dar already had. Liesel had. Jacob had.

All the lesbians in town had as well. It seemed like every gay woman Jamie knew had been in and visited. Several of the craftswomen had volunteered to lend a hand if Val needed it. Val had so far turned everyone down — at least as far as working on the project went. Jamie had no idea what Val did with her nights.

She was certain that Val would do well in the world of entertainment, where it seemed as if everyone was glib but only a few people had substance. Val had some substance. Jamie was not interested in finding out how much.

There was a knock at the back door and Liesel bustled in carrying a large basket covered by a tea towel.

"Cornbread delivery." Liesel set the basket on the counter. "I cubed it down, dear, but I didn't know if you wanted it to stay cubed or broken up."

"A little of both," Jamie said. "Just spread it out on the big cookie sheets and I'll pop them in the oven after I turn it off."

"You look beat," Liesel observed.

"Yeah, but I'm turning a profit."

"That's because she has slave labor," Val muttered.

Liesel laughed, but Jamie gave Val a narrow look. "Tonight alone, you have learned how to roast red peppers, use a Cuisinart, whip egg whites, fold egg whites and macerate raisins."

"What-erate raisins?"

"Here." Jamie handed Val an eight-cup measure two-thirds full of raisins. "Get the kettle up to a boil, then pour enough boiling water into this to cover the raisins. Let them soak for about five minutes. Let me know when time's up and I'll show you what to do next. You'll love macerating."

"Oh to be young again," Liesel said. "Not. I've always said you couldn't pay me to be young again. Thirty-nine — now that's a nice age. Ten more years for you, *liebchen*."

"When are you going to stop calling me little girl?" Jamie gave Liesel a fond look.

"When you're older than me."

A startled cry from Val made Jamie look her way.

"I didn't know the handle would be hot," Val said. She was shaking one hand and glaring at the large kettle.

Liesel tsk'd. "Put some ice on it or it'll keep burning."

"And use the oven mitts. That's why they're all over the kitchen." Jamie turned back to her mincemeat.

"It's a nuisance to always be taking them on and off."

"You wear gloves to hammer, don't you?" She did a rapid calculation, multiplying the recipe times two and a half. Three tablespoons butter became seven point five, or almost a whole stick. "Lots of people die in kitchen accidents."

"I'm not surprised."

Val's tone was so dry that Jamie had to look up. "Someone ate too many cookies for dinner."

"Someone was too busy slaving to eat anything else."

"I think I'll head on home," Liesel said. "Jamie, dear, don't you even think about making anything for our Thanksgiving dinner — I'm doing all the work so you can rest." She looked pointedly at Val, then sidled out the door with a wave good-bye.

Val was rubbing an ice cube over her palm. "You're just a fountain of joy, you know that?"

Jamie turned back to her work, refusing to be drawn into a fight. "You thought of this, not me."

"Just don't make me keep paying for it, okay?"

"And why not? If anything about life is true it's that you never pay for anything once."

"And here I was thinking you weren't philosophical."

"And here I was thinking you — oh, forget it. I'm too tired."

Val suddenly grinned. "Don't poop out on me now. I was just getting an adrenaline surge."

There is was again, that charm. "Let's call it quits after the raisins are ready. I'm seeing double and nuts are too expensive to risk."

"What is that, anyway?"

"Vegetarian mincemeat. Usually you add finely chopped meat — beef or pork. But I use almonds and walnuts. This year I'm trying hazelnuts and macadamias, too. Then you add raisins and a sugar syrup, spices, mix and fill pie crusts. I have orders for a total of twelve mincemeat pies. And fifteen pumpkin. Tomorrow you'll learn how to make a pecan paste filling for pumpkin pie."

Val yawned. "Excuse me, sorry. It's not you, but I am tired. Three more minutes on the raisins."

Jamie covered her work with clean tea towels, then went out to the dining room to turn the sign to closed and shut off the lights.

Val looked at her blearily when she returned. "Five minutes soaking in boiling water. Done."

Jamie handed Val a bowl already containing a cup of sugar and a mashing tool. "Macerating just means the raisins are softened and then gently mashed. We still want raisin shapes. Just dump a third of them in, mash a little, pick up the sugar with them — like that. You got it."

Val had the raisins ready in no time. "Just like sandy mortar," she said through another yawn.

Jamie wearily shrugged into her jacket. "See you in the morning. Are you comfortable enough upstairs? Liesel was serious about the room at her house." Liesel liked Val immensely, which irked Jamie a tetch.

"I'm fine," Val said. "It's kind of nice to be alone after the busy day."

"I know what you mean," Jamie said. "This place was never empty when I was growing up. Oh —" Jamie remembered Liesel's pointed look. "I'm suppose to invite you to Thanksgiving dinner at Liesel's."

Val quirked her lips. "Are you inviting me because Liesel made you?"

Jamie stifled a yawn. "I would have remembered around noon on Thursday, after all the food was picked up and the dishes done. My ability to think ahead is limited to ordering supplies. Take the afternoon off and come to dinner. Liesel will think I scared you off if you don't."

"We can't have that, can we?" Val lowered her gaze to the tea towel she was drying her hands on. "Tell Liesel I would be honored."

"Great," Jamie said. "Lock up after me."

"As if I'd forget," Val muttered when Jamie was gone. She locked the back door firmly and dragged herself upstairs. Who knew that cooking was every bit as tiring physically as hanging wallpaper? She'd done both today.

Her thirty-five days until Christmas were now thirty. So far she'd marked walls for demolition — placement of the fireplace in particular. There were only a few walls that weren't going to be touched, and those she had painted with a scrubbable quality white. Jamie was still making up her mind about which Shaker stenciling pattern she liked best. The wallpaper had gone into what would eventually be a master suite on the third floor, incorporating some of the existing attic. Maybe they'd get their permit to go ahead tomorrow. Maybe if Val took one of Jamie's pies down to the inspectors it would move things along. Bribery, she told herself. Bribery was not a good thing unless it worked.

She slowly stumbled out of her clothes and pulled an old T-shirt over her head. As she reached for the light she saw that the fax machine had a sheet of paper in it.

It was Sheila's itinerary. She and Mark Warnell

were arriving on Christmas Eve morning. Make that thirty days minus one, Val thought numbly. She reminded herself that everything was worth the end goal.

Just before sleep claimed her she wondered when Jamie would stop being so prickly. She could like Jamie. She'd thought her stolid, then revised her opinion to rock-steady. But there had to be a side that wasn't rock. Imagining Jamie's soft side coaxed Val into smiling sleep.

# Bread Pudding *(Innocence Lost)*

This bread pudding can be innocent, simple and low in fat, or it can be seductive (yes, seductive bread pudding!) and extremely decadent. It can be a little of both—you choose!

1/2 cup sugar
3 eggs or equivalent egg substitute
1 tsp vanilla
2-1/2 cups or any combination of nonfat to
whole milk to half-n-half, your choice.
(I often use 1 cup half-n-half and 1-1/2 cups nonfat milk)
1/2 tsp cinnamon
3 cups white bread cubes or cubed
cinnamon rolls or combination of both
1/2 cup raisins to sprinkle on top

PREPARATION:

Prepare 13x9 pan with cooking spray. Have a second pan that is slightly larger standing by. Cube the bread or cinnamon rolls and sprinkle evenly into sprayed pan. If they are really fresh, toast under the broiler for 3-5 minutes. Have a measuring cup or tea kettle with hot water ready—use something you can pour a small stream from.

CUSTARD:

Combine all other ingredients except the raisins, beating until smooth. Pour over the cubes and sprinkle top with raisins.

BAKING:

Pour hot water into the slightly larger pan (not the one with the pudding!) until the bottom is just covered. Set the pudding pan into the hot water. Don't worry if the sides touch. There just needs to be room enough for hot water to surround the pudding pan while it bakes (this prevents the custard from overcooking and sticking). Depending on how much larger the outer pan is, the hot water may rise and spill or may not fill the pan enough. Outer pan should be full of hot water to about 1/2 inch below rim.

Using hot pads (!!!) put the pans into your preheated oven. Bake approximately 55 minutes until the custard is no longer runny and doesn't jiggle. Serve cold or warm with whipped cream.

*From the Waterview, Mendocino*

# 8

When the first of Val's extra workers arrived it didn't take Jamie long to figure out that Jan had a special relationship with Val. She would have been surprised if Val didn't have a girlfriend in the offing — she was too attractive to be single.

Admitting Val was attractive was saving Jamie considerable energy. She'd wasted the best part of the week since Thanksgiving fighting the realization that Val was doing something to her composure. She'd finally given herself permission to feel Val's allure; she wasn't immune to what a whole lot of other women were finding very appealing. Okay, she felt it. But she didn't have to do anything about it.

She was tempted, though, to let Val's first attempt at baking burn. She wasn't going to speculate on what might be happening over her head at this very moment. All she knew was that Jan and Val had gone upstairs to measure and the floorboards had stopped creaking nearly ten minutes ago.

She pretended not to notice when Val finally did reappear that her cheeks were flushed, hair slightly mussed and top button of her jeans undone.

"I took them out of the oven for you."

"Thanks." Val bent over the golden loaves. "Are they supposed to crack?"

"Yes," Jamie said. "The moisture in the crack is how you check for doneness." She put down her paring knife and joined Val in examining the poppyseed loaves. "See the moisture here — that's as much as you would ever want to see. The crack should look only that moist, no more. Less moist is also okay. But you don't want it completely dry."

"Kind of like when to do the broom finish on concrete."

"Okay," Jamie said. "If that helps you remember." Broom finish?

"I want to taste one." Val picked up a nearby knife and began inserting it into one of the loaves.

"Stop that!" Jamie held back an exasperated sigh. "You'll ruin the loaf for serving. Never cut it in the pan, you get torn slices when you try to remove them. Run the knife along the outside edges, then tip the pan to the side and shake gently. If you used enough shortening on the sides it should slip right — there."

"Now can I have a slice?"

126

Val's pleading eyes were the color of the rolling ocean on a sunny day. Jamie shook away the fanciful comparison. "Yes, but get a serrated knife. Now slice your piece with only three passes of the knife."

"Huh?"

"Only go back and forth a total of three times. Back, forth, back. That's all."

"You're picky."

"Do it your way, then."

Val sawed off a slice and Jamie was only slightly satisfied when the adjacent piece tore. "Okay, I see your point. We can't serve that piece now."

"Three passes is usually enough and it's a good guide to how much pressure to use. The knife also has to be sharp enough."

Val cut the torn slice away using Jamie's method. "I see. Back, forth, back, and it's done." She took a big bite of her slice. "Wow, that's good. I can't believe I did it myself. Your recipe is dynamite."

"It's the standard *Joy of Cooking* recipe," Jamie said. "With a little more poppyseed than they call for."

Jan came into the kitchen looking almost — but not quite — as neat as she had when she'd gone upstairs.

"Hey, try this," Val said. "I made it."

Jan nibbled on the piece Val proffered. Jamie turned away from the eye contact the two were making. Big deal.

"That's really good. You made it all by yourself? I didn't know you were a chef, too."

Jamie snorted and turned it into a cough. She had better get used to hearing that.

Val was hemming and hawing. "Well, Jamie has taught me a lot."

"I'm ready to start on the master bath wall." Jan licked her fingers — Jamie assumed it wasn't just for crumbs, then kicked herself mentally for being catty.

Another of the workers clomped into the kitchen. Val served up another slice of poppyseed loaf. The newcomer looked too much like Jan to be anything but a brother. "I feel like knocking down a wall," he said, after wolfing down the slice of cake.

The three of them disappeared upstairs and soon there was the most gawdawful racket Jamie had ever heard. She concentrated on cubing cinnamon rolls for bread pudding, but she cringed at every blow. She could feel each one resonating in her feet and wondered if the house could stand it.

Val reappeared sometime later, covered in some sort of dust. "It's going great," she informed Jamie with a big smile.

The woman really did like knocking down a wall more than kneading bread dough. Takes all kinds, Jamie thought.

"Your walls are in good shape. I don't see any sign of dry rot or infestations. We'll have an inspector out here tomorrow morning, I'd say. They're really responsive, which is great. I think it'll be the same guy as last time — he really dug that mincemeat pie."

"Save him some of your poppyseed loaf. Serve it with a dollop of the cranberry jam on the side. Big cup of coffee — one attitude-adjustment snack done."

"Attitude adjustment," Val echoed. "Sounds so much better than bribe. Hey, what's this?"

"Bread pudding made with cinnamon rolls instead of bread."

"Can I have some after dinner?" Val swung across the kitchen and Jamie noticed for the first time that she was wearing a tool belt. It sat low on her hips and for some reason made Jamie feel — well, warm. No, that was just the stove. What was a tool belt to her? It wasn't as if she was into butch women. Kathy was hardly butch.

Of course, she wasn't into Kathy anymore, so there was no telling what her libido might decide. At the moment her libido was babbling about Val's legs, and her brain was contemplating something delectable that would substitute for Val. Something very, very, deeply and darkly, richly, comfortingly chocolate.

Peanut butter cake. With fudge topping.

Val went upstairs again and Jamie's brain took a trip to chocolate land. She stirred the daily special — pork and sweet potato stew — and imagined herself swimming in milk chocolate. The hint of cinnamon, the cream — she could feel it on her face, her cheeks, in her hair, she gasped for air — the scent of it filling her nose as she sought to devour all she could, sensing the strength of Val's legs around her . . .

Wait a minute.

Val was in her chocolate fantasy. That would simply not do.

Jamie quickly assessed the status of the primary lunch offerings. They were all okay. The week after Thanksgiving week was proving slow.

Cocoa powder, heavy cream, graham crackers, peanut butter, eggs, butter, flour, baker's chocolate, more butter, chocolate chips, the double boiler, medium springform pan, sifter, grinder, cinnamon, vanilla . . .

She made the peanut butter cake in record time. She made it like she hadn't made it in years. As if she'd been waiting all her life to make that cake, right then and there. She paced while it cooled, then melted chocolate and whipped it into warmed heavy cream. She poured the thick, sensual fudge over the still warm cake, where it pooled in luscious rich puddles that slowly dripped down the cake's sides to gather in gleaming, tempting layers.

When it was done Jamie sat down, worn out. Having a slice seemed like sacrilege. She wanted to look at it for a long time, then perhaps steal a swipe of the fudge, lick it from her fingers.

Only the smell of rolls on the verge of burning brought her out of her reverie. She'd filled Dar's orders automatically while making it, but the last few minutes had been spent in fervent contemplation.

She felt calm inside. She felt much better.

Then Val came back, still wearing her tool belt.

Jamie had a slice of cake the moment Val left.

"If I didn't know better I'd say your thoughts are someplace else." Jan rolled over in bed, but it was too dark for Val to see her expression.

"I'm sorry, where were we?" Val let her hand wander down Jan's thigh again.

"We don't have to if you don't want to. Really. What's bothering you?"

Val thought about it. "Nothing, really. I'm tired, of course."

"Who wouldn't be? You're putting in twelve hours a day. Eight hours on construction, another four in the kitchen. How much of this place do you own?"

"None," Val admitted.

"How much can she be paying you?" Jan sounded very puzzled.

"Uh, not a dime for my time."

"I see," Jan said. She plainly did not.

"Have you ever read my column?"

"All the time. That's why I jumped at the chance to do that video thing."

"Exactly where do I live and what does it look like?"

"Well, it's someplace big, with lots of wood pieces and beautiful decorating, with a big kitchen and . . . well, fabulous."

"What would you think if I said I lived in a one-bedroom apartment on the verge of falling down that I've never done a lick of work to."

"Well, I've seen you in action. You've certainly renovated something."

Val smiled to herself. "Lots of somethings. Just nothing of my own."

"So what's up with this inn?"

"Well . . ." It sounded so silly. "Warnell Communications wants to make me their expert on home and garden and renovation. And the CEO wants to make sure I'm the real thing."

"Oh." Jan was trying not to laugh, Val could tell. "You have to show something off."

"If it works I'll be rich and famous."

"I can say I knew you when. That I slept with you when."

"It sounds so absurd. And so vapid. I mean, I *do* want to be rich and famous. Who wouldn't? But I really want to build things, and make them beautiful, and show women in particular what my father taught me every day of my life — don't settle. If you want something to change, change it yourself. I don't have to be rich and famous to do that, but a little bit of fame wouldn't hurt. And some capital to buy something, renovate it and sell it again."

"So why this place? So far off the beaten track?"

"Oh. Well, I don't really know how to cook much. Jamie's teaching me." It was a bit of a relief to tell someone the whole truth.

"She is a good cook," Jan said. "Okay, so you made a trade. But I think she's getting the best of it."

"Probably," Val agreed. "But while the people from Warnell are here she's going to fade into the background and let me take all the credit for everything. I've learned a lot, but I can't do the cooking myself."

"Well, that's something." Jan stretched. "I suppose after you're famous I won't see you again. You'll be off to New York or someplace ritzy."

"It doesn't have to be that way," Val protested.

"But it will be. Hey, it's okay. I'm not the marrying kind, and I don't think you are either."

Val was both relieved and bothered. Jan as usual was stealing her lines. She accepted that they were just having fun — spectacular fun. But how could Jan be so sure Val wasn't the marrying kind? "I hope to keep in touch." She brushed her fingertips over Jan's ribs, then yawned.

"Yeah, yeah," Jan said. "Go to sleep."


Jamie found that she could reduce her stress level by simply ignoring all the work going on around her. She knew that Jan and Stan were on their last day, having been brought on primarily to help with the largest demolition and rebuilding. Well, Val had found other uses for Jan, Jamie reminded herself, then gave herself yet another lecture on cattiness, a trait Aunt Em had deplored.

She found it best not to look at the new fireplace in the dining room, or even to go up to the master bedroom. She'd never thought of it as a master bedroom, but it would soon sport a large bath with a clawfoot tub and, according to Val, a bay window with an ocean view and a small pellet stove that provided extra heat and the romance of a small, clean flame to fall asleep by.

She supposed that when Val was done it would be her own room, and that she ought to be taking more of an interest in what was being done to it. She'd picked the Shaker patterns she liked and helped decide on the tables, benches and chairs. Val had access to some fabulous pricing, too. She had never dreamed of anything as extensive as Val's vision, nor thought she could afford it. But the bank had been willing to make a small capital improvements loan, and so far the interest payments wouldn't bankrupt her because she hadn't had to borrow as much as she had thought. She had good security to offer in the Waterview, so the interest rate was a bit easier to swallow.

Still, she kept her head down, tried to ignore Val's charm, enthusiasm, hips, eyes, and she made a lot of chocolate.

Chocolate soufflé, chocolate ice cream, chocolate blackout cake, chocolate raspberry mousse, chocolate cream pie, chocolate pastilles, chocolate dipped orange peels, chocolate chip cookies, chocolate hazelnut pie on chocolate chip graham cracker crust, chocolate cherry buckle, milk chocolate chip pie, pound cake with chocolate custard cream filling, Hungarian chocolate,

133

chocolate bark, praline chocolate clusters — and just for a change she'd pop a Snickers miniature in her mouth with her afternoon cup of coffee. Thank God she could sell all the chocolate she was making after having a small sample herself.

Chocolate versus Valkyrie Valentine, Jamie thought. Until now she'd have said chocolate would win versus anything.

She finished swirling together the ingredients for a hearty quiche — the morning breakfast special — and pulled out her latest chocolate muffins. An inspector was due any minute to check the fireplaces and upstairs wallboard. All the inspectors had formed a habit of starting in the kitchen where Jamie usually just happened to have a tasty something and a cup of coffee handy.

Sure enough, muffins and coffee disappeared upstairs with Val and inspector. A friend of Jeff O'Rhuan's was making a clatter in the stairwell, running new electrical wiring while the walls were missing. Val had been pleased to find a licensed electrician, and Jamie kept him supplied with food throughout the day. She had just finished pressing a big slice of quiche on him when she realized that Liesel was right — Aunt Em would be proud of the way things were changing and what Jamie was doing. Feeding people, making herself happy. For she was happy.

It was a happiness with limits. Obviously someone to share this happiness with would be nice. A little passion, a little laughter — it would be very nice. Kathy was right out, she believed that now. The problem was reminding herself that Val was right out, too.

She had a sliver of chocolate bark.

When the inspector came back downstairs he looked happy. He thanked her as always for the coffee and treat. They proceeded on to the dining room.

Val said over her shoulder, "You can come look, too, you know." She needn't have had such a knowing smile, Jamie thought.

When she finally took in the enormity of the changes, she was glad that Val was occupied with the inspector. The room was so different she almost felt like it wasn't her inn anymore. The walls that had been repainted were now sea foam white. The ceiling was even whiter, making it appear to soar higher above the room than its nine feet. With wide unembellished facings and mantels, the fireplace dominated the far wall. The lines were clean and there wasn't a scallop or curlicue in sight.

The fireplace was actually three smaller fireplaces with one common mantel. Each was up off the floor about two feet with bench-type hearth in front where a person could warm her backside. Each was gas-powered with special reflectors to increase both the heat output and glow. Val assured Jamie that when they were running she wouldn't need any other heat in the dining room, especially after they insulated under the old wood floor. Insulation would come after the floor was refinished and the Warnell party had come and gone.

She liked it. Liked it very much. Without Val's artistic eye she would never have seen how these simple lines could add so much ambiance and style. She pictured the wood tables already on order fitted out with simple condiment trays and plates full of *her* food. Her finest stews and breads, cacciatores and pastas — and best of all, her aunt's special cherry pie with ribbon crust.

Teary-eyed, she backed out of the room and found privacy in the walk-in refrigerator. Not enough, though, because Val tracked her down a few minutes later.

"Why are you hiding out in here?"

Jamie busied herself counting milk cartons. "I'm busy."

"Yeah. Well — I thought . . . Fine. Just fine." Val turned on her heel.

"Wait." Jamie scrubbed her eyes with her apron.

"What's wrong?" Jamie tried not to notice that Val's eyes were like liquid cobalt. "You hate it. I thought you were waiting to be surprised or I'd have made you really look at it sooner. You hate it."

"I love it. I'm crying because I love it. I cry when I'm happy."

"You're not making that up, are you?"

Jamie shook her head. "My aunt would love it, too. You know I had misgivings about all of this —"

"That's putting it mildly."

"Well, you've held up your end of the bargain more than I ever thought possible." Jamie had to say it, even if Val was smiling in the way that made her want lots and lots of chocolate. "And I'll throw my heart into holding up mine."

"Friends, then? Finally?" Val held out her hand.

Even in the cold air of the refrigerator, Jamie felt the warmth of Val's fingertips right down into her thighs. "Friends, then."

They shook on it. Jamie wondered if Val's way of stretching the truth had worn off — her feelings were beyond friendly.

Mendocino was not easy to get to, not without a helicopter. I wasted hours driving to the place. The whole trip was probably pointless. I had far too much to do because of the holidays — everyone knows that no work is transacted in New York during the last two weeks of December, and Dallas is almost as bad. So I really couldn't afford to make this trip.

But I had to. Whenever we talked, my father spoke of little else besides how much he was looking forward to an intimate holiday with all the traditional trimmings. He had no idea the pressure he was putting on me, and I needed to put some of that pressure on Ms. Valentine. I needed to be sure that everything was going to be okay, because if it wasn't my father would likely never forgive me, and likely never give me a chance like this again.

I had carte blanche with the media relations and art departments. We had scores of logos, six possibilities for a theme song, an entire book of studio sketches. Number crunchers were cranking out revenue projections every time I sneezed. A few days ago I realized that if Val and I didn't come to a business agreement I'd have so much egg on my face I could open my own breakfast place. Somehow it had gotten away from me. VV — Valkyrie Valentine — had taken on a life of its own.

The town was charming enough. Wood sidewalks, lots of artists' boutiques. There was no neon. While there were definitely some buildings turned out for tourist conceptions of picturesque, they were still in keeping with the general feeling of the place. There was no sign of any new buildings done in faux historical architecture. I hate that. The wooden sidewalks weren't for show — the streets showed signs of mud and flash flooding recently.

It had been raining in Dallas when I left. I hadn't seen the sun in almost two weeks. So this sun, gleaming on the ocean and white cliffs, was dazzling. I almost didn't see the sign for Val's Waterview house as I drove slowly down the main street. It was after lunch, but I was sure I could convince Val to give me a meal.

I parked the rental car and then spotted a small bookstore. I'd run out of reading material on the plane and had been disgusted with my choices at the airport gift shop. I decided to duck into this bookstore first, while it was open, and find something to read. I didn't feel right unless I was in the middle of a book.


Jamie munched on a chocolate wafer and leaned against the back door. The fog was late coming in, but this was going to be her only lull in the afternoon. Her gaze was caught by a petite woman in a very short, blinding yellow suit. Ball earrings in Halloween orange dangled from her ears. From the back her red beehive was impressive. Jamie rolled her eyes. Tourists.

As she went back inside she discovered Val trying to scrub paint off her T-shirt. She was swearing.

"Can I help?"

"No. It never fails that a little tiny project becomes a great big one. You should see the floor upstairs. I was just touching up the trim when I dumped over the can."

"That's sad."

The look Val gave her made Jamie want to giggle. She enjoyed seeing Val discomfited for once. She had paint in her hair.

"Your hair's okay," Jamie added. "You could hide the painted parts in a beehive. I just saw a tourist with a beehive do. Maybe they're back in style."

"This is my favorite T-shirt," Val muttered. "I was only going to paint one little thing. No need — a tourist with *what*?"

Jamie was taken aback by Val's sudden intensity. "She was headed for the bookstore. Bright yellow suit. I'll bet her shirt is white with black polka dots."

"Red hair?"

"Yeah. And a bright yellow . . . what's wrong."

Val had gone pale. Then she bolted to the back door. "Which way did she go?"

"Down the block. Why?"

"She wouldn't surprise me, would she? I'm just paranoid." Val stood on tiptoe, then slithered onto the back porch behind the big bougainvillea.

Jamie decided it was time to get back to cooking. She stirred the thick beef stew and tasted it. It lacked depth. She rummaged amongst the bottles next to the stove and finally added about twelve ounces of a full-bodied cabernet sauvignon.

A heartfelt and long-pronounced swear word floated in from the back porch. A few seconds later Val flew by Jamie and on up the stairs. "Don't say anything. You don't speak English. Ply her with coffee, just don't say anything." From the first floor landing Jamie heard, "Shit shit shit . . ." until it faded out. There was a loud thud followed by some furious scrabbling and then the one working shower started.

Jamie kept an eye out and sure enough a few moments later the redhead, looking a little puzzled, came into the dining room. She stopped Dar, who was on her way to a table with two plates of pie. Dar nodded in the direction of the kitchen. Jamie ducked out of sight and stirred the stew as if it took one hundred percent of her concentration. She didn't think the redhead would be fooled. The water stopped upstairs.

"Excuse me, I'm looking for Val Valentine? Am I in the right place?"

"She's upstairs at the moment."

"I didn't know she ran a café."

"Well, as you can see it's undergoing some major changes."

"That's clear." The redhead looked confused. "Should I look for her upstairs?"

"I'm sure she'll be right back down. She . . . was going to taste the stew. I don't think I have it the way she wanted. Would you like some coffee?"

"That would be great."

Jamie poured a cup, betting that the redhead would find it weak. She looked as if she could do a direct IV of Liesel's strong brew — she had that thin, slightly nervous look of a caffeine junkie.

Val was coming down the stairs. Jamie stepped back and said in what she hoped was a subservient tone, "There's someone here to see you." She blinked at Val's pristine navy slacks and Edwardian linen shirt, and she reached instinctively into the cupboard where the clean aprons were stacked.

Val's eyes telegraphed a thank you as she tossed the neck loop over her head and tied the waist cord in Jamie's habitual back-front-back method, finished with a bowtie. Val took a deep breath, then seemed to catch the newcomer out of the corner of her eye.

"Sheila! What a wonderful surprise! What, you couldn't wait for shrimp scampi?"

Jamie whistled to herself, then went back to stirring the stew. So . . . this was Sheila Thintowski. The woman with Val's future in the palm of her hand. Eccentric dresser. Well, Jamie, she reminded herself, you promised Val you'd give it your all.

The two were exchanging hugs and then Sheila burst into a flurry of questions about the inn, the renovations and first and foremost, why Val hadn't told Sheila that there was so much work underway.

For just a moment, Val looked at a loss for words, then she said with grace of a true hostess, "Let's get comfortable and take our coffee into the other room."

Sheila began to protest.

Jamie interrupted Shiela with a quiet, "Val? Before you go I need you to okay the stew."

"Oh yes," Val said. She turned away from Sheila and mouthed, "Help me!"

Jamie picked up one of the French loaves. "I've been practicing hollowing these out like you told me." She deftly extracted the core of the bread to make a suitable bread bowl for the stew. "Is that right?"

"Yes, you've got it." Val then took the spoon Jamie

proffered and tasted the stew. "It's got a really good flavor, but you know, I think it needs salt, of all things. Good old ordinary salt."

Jamie was not about to add salt without tasting it herself, but she nodded and said, "Right away."

"Let's move out to the dining room," Val said to Sheila. Her color was back and from the bounce in her step, Jamie had a feeling that Val had found just the right explanation for Sheila.

Jamie tasted the stew. Damn. It did need salt.

## Cornbread & Sausage Stuffing

This stuffing is a down home change from traditional sage and celery. It is delicious by itself, stuffed in pork or chicken. The roasted red pepper gives it a unique, memorable flavor.

> 1/2 pound sausage, your choice (I usually select lean pork)
> 1 yellow or red onion, diced
> 2 cups crumbled stale cornbread or cornbread stuffing mix
> 1/2 - 3/4 cup chicken stock (canned is fine, look for low salt)
> 1 red pepper, roasted (see below)

PREPARATION:
Cut the red pepper into quarters and remove stem, seeds and inner white membranes. Place skin up on a foil-covered cookie sheet. Put under a high broiler until the skin is blackened. Shake the pepper slices from the aluminum foil into a brown paper bag and close tightly. When the peppers are cool (at least 15 minutes) remove all of the blackened skin (it should come right off) and chop into small pieces.
While the peppers are cooling, remove sausage from casings, if necessary, then fry and crumble. When sausage is done remove from pan to paper towels to drain. Pour off any accumulated fat from pan, but don't scrape, and then sauté the onion in the same pan until translucent.

METHOD:
Thoroughly mix cornbread, cooked sausage and onion, roasted peppers and 1/2 cup of chicken stock. For a side dish, place in a baking dish that can be tightly covered. If you like stuffing moist, pour another 1/4 cup chicken stock over the top and stir. Cover dish and bake at 325° for about 30 minutes, until heated through. If you like the top crunchy, uncover, drizzle with a little melted butter and put under the broiler until golden.
If used to stuff a whole chicken, do not add the additional 1/4 cup stock. Pack the body cavity loosely. I have tried this stuffing in turkey and it works, but it's better in chicken or game hens.
If stuffing chicken breasts or pork chops, add the extra 1/4 cup chicken stock before stuffing and mix thoroughly.

**⫶⫶⫶⫶⫶⫶ From the Waterview, Mendocino ⫶⫶⫶⫶⫶⫶**

# 9

A lie plus a lie does not equal truth. Val decided to tell Sheila the truth — just not the whole truth.

"After you called and said that Mark Warnell wanted to be my Christmas guest, I thought, well, I really wanted to impress him. I just knew I had to finish the rest of the projects here by then, so that's what I've been doing."

Sheila was still frowning. "But why is this actually open for business? Since when do you run a restaurant?"

"It was only very recently that I became involved with the Waterview. The restaurant was already here."

"But I thought you said you lived here. That you only had an apartment in San Francisco. I mean — I'm confused. Just where have you done all the projects you write about?"

Val had hoped Sheila wouldn't ask point blank. But she had. *Oy vey*. "Can I be candid? I wasn't sure how you would react, so I didn't volunteer it before. But I see that was a mistake." Val tried her most innocent look. "If we're to be partners, then I should be completely forthcoming."

Sheila was still frowning. "Go on."

"The projects I wrote about were for other people. I didn't have the capital to do them all for myself. But I was longing to really do something for myself. So I settled here. And with the help of friends and a —" Val stopped to clear her throat — "good assistant chef, I was able to make a lot of headway on an antiquated building." Okay, so she was still clinging to the lie that she could cook. Well, she sort of could now. With Jamie's help. She could make Cheerios.

"So this is all your work?"

Val felt a swell of pride, and she answered with complete honesty. "My conception and, except for the heavy work, all my own."

"Very nice. But are you going to be finished in time?" Sheila's frown had finally dissolved. She looked more like the woman Val had met in San Francisco whose eyes held an endless come hither.

"Yes," Val said. "Oh yes. The renovation will be done by then. This used to be an inn, guest rooms upstairs and everything. We're enlarging the master suite, redecorating the other family bedrooms on the same floor, then eliminating two guest rooms to add two full baths and one water closet. Can you believe they expected eight people to share two bathrooms?"

Sheila looked incredulous. "And they made money? Were they nuts?"

A shadow fell over Val's shoulder and Val hoped it wasn't Jamie.

It was. Val hoped Jamie didn't take Sheila's remark personally.

"I've only just finished writing up your notes from our menu discussion. Am I right in guessing that this lady is one of that party?"

Criminees, Jamie sounded so meek, so . . . inexperienced. Val felt a real pang of guilt as she took the paper Jamie was handing to her with a meaningful glance.

"Yes, she is. Sheila, this is Jamie Onassis, the best chef assistant in the world."

"Any relation?" Val noticed Sheila didn't offer to shake hands.

Jamie blinked. "No. At least, I don't think so. No oil, no money here."

Sheila smiled dismissively and Val decided right about then that she didn't like Sheila much. Nevertheless, she found some enthusiasm. "This is what I was thinking for our Christmas Day meal." She scanned the page quickly. "Yes, I think it's all here. A Jane Austen menu. Of course, the whole time you're here the dining room will be closed, so we'll have it to ourselves. Candlelight, the sound system will be working again by then, so conceptually you should be thinking Handel or Bach for music. We'll start with Winter Pease Soup and Vegetable Pie." She had no doubt that the vegetable pie would be complete with Jamie's melt-in-your-mouth crust.

Jamie cut in smoothly with, "Val was telling me that in Austen's time a formal meal was served what we call family-style, that is, food on the table and passed around as necessary. It wasn't until later than formal dining meant food cut on a sideboard and delivered finished, like in a restaurant. She thought the Austen era was more intimate."

"My — Mark Warnell loves Jane Austen. He's going to be thrilled."

"Don't tell him in advance," Val said. "I don't want to ruin the surprise — or raise his expectations so high I can't meet them."

"Okay," Sheila said. "I'll keep the secret." She seemed thoroughly convinced of the need for secrecy and Val felt much, much better about carrying it all off.

This is, until she looked at the menu again. "Jamie, I can't quite read your writing." She pointed.

"I'm sorry that's so sloppy." Jamie was getting better at subterfuge. "That's the Celery Ragout with Wine."

Ra-goo? Val had almost said rag-out. She pointed at the next item. "And this?"

"Pheasant *à la braise* with Forcemeat Balls."

"Oh yes, the pheasant. I think you'll like this roasting method." She said *roasting* with some confidence, since Jamie had written it next to the name and underlined it. "And an egg dish, they were big on eggs in those days."

"Val has been so nice to me," Jamie said. "She

said I can help out with the meal, and I'll learn how to make a Syllabub."

Jamie was really throwing herself into this, Val thought. She'd anticipated Val's problem with whatever a Syllabub was. She was breathlessly describing some sugar concoction flavored with wine. Sounded awful, actually.

She was about to offer her own observation when she saw Dar headed their way. Cheezit. Dar could give away the whole shebang.

Jamie was already heading her off. The two conversed briefly, then Jamie, from behind Sheila, pointed at herself and made an urgent gesture toward the kitchen.

Val sighed contentedly to Sheila. "Jamie is a godsend. She can handle tonight's menu just fine on our own, in fact it's her own recipe for cornbread stuffing in game hens —"

"So we could have a chance to get to know each other," Sheila said.

Oops. "I wish I could offer you a place to stay, but all the rooms are torn up," Val said. She had a perfectly good idea where Sheila had expected to stay, but she was too afraid of slipping up to even consider making an offer of her bed. Besides, Sheila's high wattage sex appeal was increasingly unappealing. "It's very primitive at the moment."

Sheila was plainly disappointed. "Maybe I could offer you something more civilized for the evening, then."

"It would be . . . difficult. I don't usually call it a day until after eleven, and I'm up by five-thirty in the morning."

"And your assistant couldn't cover you so you could have a . . . late morning?"

"I wish she could," Val lied. It wasn't hard — she was getting a tad tired of Sheila's assumption that Val could be bedded so easily. Did she give off that kind of vibe?

She was so intent on ducking Sheila that Liesel's hand on her shoulder made her jump.

"Jamie finally let you have a seat?"

"Finally." This is it, Val thought. She felt as if she were in a drawing-room murder scene, and all the fingers were going to start pointing at her.

"Cooking lessons can be very draining," was all Liesel said. "Well, I didn't mean to interrupt, just wanted to say hello."

Val felt faint with relief. She was not cut out for a life of deception.

"Just how many gay women are there in this town?"

Val grinned. "Enough. It's a very artsy live-and-let-live kind of town."

"I could spend some time here," Sheila said coyly. "So your assistant is demanding. Is that all she is?"

"What?" Val stared at Sheila, confused. Then she caught the innuendo. "Oh, no. No — Jamie and me, no, that's not in the cards." She laughed.

Jamie appeared out of nowhere. How did she do that? Val choked on the laugh and tried to fathom Jamie's expression. Had she heard? Well, if she had she showed no signs of emotion, and she was pretty easy to read, all in all. Right now she just looked blank.

"This is Val's new blend of coffee. I thought you might like to try it." Jamie set the cup down in front of Sheila and walked away, her back straight as a broomstick. It was always like that. Was Jamie mad? Val couldn't tell, which bothered her.

"Maybe you can show me the town," Sheila was saying. "I have to drive back to the airport tomorrow, so this will be my chance to plan some sightseeing for Mr. Warnell."

"I'd be glad to," Val said. She would do almost anything to get Sheila out of the place.

Val went to the kitchen to take off her apron. Jamie was chopping nuts like there was no tomorrow. "I'm going to show Sheila the sights and hopefully park her at Hillside House." Hillside House was the hotel farthest away. Sheila might be intrigued by the fact that the *Murder, She Wrote* cast had often stayed there when doing filming in "Cabot Cove."

Jamie said, "That sounds good," over her shoulder, but she never stopped chopping the nuts.

"Making anything special?" Jamie had been turning out a delicious chocolate concoction every night for nearly two weeks now.

"Hazelnut Charlotte. I don't feel like chocolate right now."

"Sounds great." Val headed out the door, glad that Jamie was not angry with her.


Jamie was off chocolate. Val's laughing rebuttal of the notion that she and Jamie could have any relationship had taken care of her infatuation. It would be a cold day in Hell before she made chocolate anything over Valkyrie Valentine. Absurd name, anyway.

151

Jamie supposed that she would have developed an infatuation for any reasonably presentable lesbian in close quarters with her. After all, she had only been with one woman — not even a lesbian, in retrospect. And that had been a very, very long time ago. All the pheromones that Val generated in the local lesbian population were making temperatures run a bit high, that was all.

Sheila left the next day without asking any more difficult questions. During the following week Jamie left Val to paint the dining room after the final inspections, and to continue breaking down bedroom walls. A local plumber ran new copper pipes for the extra bathrooms and replaced some existing lead pipes that might leak in the next few years. How Val managed to get them to do so much work for so little was a miracle, but they all did. Perhaps she was promising them a thank you in her first book through Warnell Communications.

Her muddled feelings didn't stop her from creating more menus for the Warnell visit. She decided on a cold meal for Christmas eve, followed by participation in the caroling that Mendocinians liked to do, followed by mulled cider and hot pumpkin loaves. Val was leery of letting Warnell mingle with townspeople, any one of whom might mention Jamie's wonderful cooking. But Jamie had argued that isolation might make them curious. Besides, caroling was a delightful tradition here, as was the early-morning Christmas service at the non-denominational church.

With Val helping in the kitchen one night Jamie arrived home a little earlier than usual and was glad of the time to just relax and talk to Liesel. KatzinJam greeted her coldly, as if Jamie had abandoned him.

She finally coaxed Katz onto her lap. "I know, buddy. I've been really busy. But soon you'll be king of the hill, in a brand new place." KatzinJam sank his claws in through Jamie's jeans, then released them. Just a little pain to let her know he was still mad, but not so much that the breach couldn't be mended. She started scratching KatzinJam's ears and worked her way to his ruff.

"Making you pay?" Liesel brought Jamie her nightly cup of hot chocolate and then sank into the sofa beside her.

"He's upset. But I was glad to get away a little earlier tonight."

"You're wearing yourself to a wisp." Liesel tsk'd maternally. "Do you think after Val leaves you'll be able to take Mondays off until tourist season?"

A logical question, but one Jamie couldn't answer. She was stuck on "after Val leaves."

"Jamie?"

"Sorry, I keep forgetting that Val will leave." She felt Liesel's searching gaze on her.

"She will. No sense thinking otherwise."

"No sense at all," Jamie echoed.

They chatted about anything but the inn and Val, then Liesel wisely suggested Jamie get a little extra sleep. She tried, but after studying the ceiling for too long, her sleep was not particularly restful.

She felt tired and heavy-lidded the next day but managed to keep up with a bustling breakfast crowd. If this continued, she'd have to take the soufflés off the menu. They took too much time, unlike her Pie Duet — a wedge of quiche with ingredients that changed every day, and a slice of Breakfast Pie. It was a popular combination.

She was beating eggs for a new batch of cobblers and bread pudding when a woman in the dining room caught her eye. Her hair was white and silver, and Jamie had the distinct impression that its becoming contrast to the denim jeans and gray sweatshirt was an accident. She was thin, ascetic almost, but not anorexic, and wore no ornamentation or rings, no watch or designer labels. She was tanned, but not deeply, and the hands that curved around the coffee cup showed signs of a lifetime of labor.

There was something familiar about her. It was as if she'd passed through the Waterview years ago. Jamie tried to picture the woman younger, then shrugged the fancy off. She would probably half-recognize lots of people over time.

The woman paid for her coffee and left, but she turned back to peer through the glass for a moment. Jamie caught the sweeping gaze of hazel eyes that probably hadn't lit up in laughter for years. She couldn't breathe. Her heart stopped beating.

She didn't remember setting the spatula down, or even hurrying through the dining room to the wooden sidewalk.

"Wait."

The woman turned back. She didn't seem surprised or dismayed.

"I'm Jamie." What would she say to that, Jamie wondered. She had wondered about this moment for many years.

"I know."

They stared at each other. Jamie tried to draw some understanding of this woman who had left her in the care of strangers over twenty-five years ago.

The long-banked anger and anguish was ready to be tapped, but the woman's — her mother's — blank response was not what Jamie had expected. Defensiveness, contrition, maybe.

At last her mother spoke. "You'll want to know why."

"I know why." Jamie said it without heat; it was the truth.

"Of course you do. You knew me better than I did m'self."

A slight drawl. She didn't sound like she did in Jamie's memories. "Then I'll ask how you could do it."

"It wasn't hard. I know you expect me to say that it was, but it wasn't. And it being so easy — that's the greatest regret of my life. That I had so little love to give that I used it all up so quickly."

"Why did you even have me?"

"I was too scared to get an abortion."

The breath left Jamie's lungs as if she'd been punched in the stomach. The ringing in her ears took several minutes to clear. When she could, she managed, "Am I supposed to thank you?"

"No. That I have a hollow soul is my concern. You were unfinished business. I had to make the effort to find out how you'd managed, settle the past so I can look at my future."

"And you were going to leave without a word? Not even an explanation?"

The hazel eyes didn't waver. They weren't serene, but resigned. "I took one look at you and knew you were Jamie, and I knew you weren't unfinished business. You're about as finished a person as I've ever seen. You know who you are. In time you'll like who you are better. And you'll be happier than I ever was or probably ever will be."

"Are you ill?"

Finally, a slight smile. "No, just leaving the world forever, not physically, but emotionally and mentally. The place where I've been the last ten years is a good retreat. I help the Sisters with the planting and harvest, and they say I'm good with the animals, though it's so easy I don't know why it deserves praise. I can't take vows because I don't believe in God." Again the slight smile. "They despair of me for that. But I can stay there for the rest of my life. I was never meant to be in the world."

"But you were long enough to have me."

"I think that was a good thing. I was meant to have you. And meant to leave you here. She raised you well."

"She was a great mother." Jamie couldn't hide a smolder of resentment.

"You deserved that. I know you don't think I have a right to, but I think I can take away some pride in the fine woman you've become."

"Am I supposed to forgive all now?"

"No. No, Jamie. You don't have to forgive me. You don't have to love me or think kindly of me. I don't deserve it." The hazel gaze turned inward. "I've been numb for twenty years and don't expect it to get any better."

Jamie took a deep breath, separating herself mentally from her mother's passivity. "Who hurt you? Why are you so wounded?"

The blankness parted and Jamie glimpsed a moment of turmoil in her mother's eyes. "I used to think I was wounded. I used to think I had scars that ran deep. It's taken me a long, long time to realize there's nothing deep about me. I'm broken, I don't know why. When I stopped searching for great joy I lost my great sadness. I was no fit mother for you. A child needs joy. There's none in me."

Jamie tried to blink back the tears, but it was no good. One after another slowly trickled down her cheeks. "I'm sorry for you, then. I don't hate you." She would never understand her mother's emptiness and had always known it had nothing to do with her. "And thank you for letting me find joy here. I never called her mother." She didn't know why she added the last, but an aching knot inside eased when her mother's eyes misted. "And I remember. I remember we laughed sometimes." She took a deep breath and dashed the tears off her cheeks. "Will you come back?"

"I don't think so. Our house is on a reservation in New Mexico and it was hard to do this. I miss it so. But here —" She held out a card to Jamie. "This is the address. You can write me, let me know how you're doing. I might not write back, but I'll read your letters. And I'll cling to my pride in you."

Jamie took the card, then glanced back at her mother. "Safe journey, then." Aunt Em had always said that when people left.

"Thank you, Jamie." She turned away.

"If you ever need anything . . ." Jamie watched her mother walk to the corner, then lost sight of her. She didn't know if her mother had even heard her. She glanced at the card in her hand, then slipped it into her pocket.

"You okay?"

She turned sharply and focused on Val. "Yeah. I'm fine."

"You're a lousy liar. What am I going to do with you?"

Jamie sniffed and realized she didn't want to go back inside through the dining room. Better to go around the back, blow her nose and try to get a sense of reality. She knew Val was following her but wasn't prepared for Val's hand on her shoulder.

It wasn't fair that every nerve in her body jumped. "Hey." She jerked out from under Val's hand.

"Don't blow me off. You're about as fine as a foggy afternoon."

"I don't want to talk about it." Val couldn't possibly empathize.

"I understand. I wouldn't want to talk. If my mother walked through that door right now I wouldn't talk to anyone about how it made me feel."

"How did you know it was my mother?"

"You look just like her. Except your eyes. Your eyes are . . . alive."

Jamie blinked and finally processed what Val had said. "Your mother abandoned you?"

"After a fashion."

"No, she either did or didn't."

"Emotionally she abandoned me when I was born. Physically, when I was seven. I grew up on army bases. I think that's why I can't cook. I really do think fried chicken is baked and corn should be shriveled, and all served up on aluminum trays."

Jamie sighed, unable to find a polite laugh at Val's attempt to cheer her up. "I don't hate her. I thought I did, at least a little. I guess I knew even then it was for the best. I wouldn't be here, otherwise." She sniffed and took a deep breath. "You wouldn't be trying to turn me into a good liar." She caught of whiff of something from the kitchen. "And I wouldn't have just burnt two cobblers and a bread pudding."

"I thought it was supposed smell like that or I'd have taken them out. The apple dessert at the PX always smelled like that."

Jamie rolled her eyes. "Let's have another cooking lesson. How to tell when something is done."

She would think about her mother later. She still felt the imprint of Val's hand on her shoulder. She would think about that later, too.


Val hadn't thought about her mother in a long time. She tossed and turned under the comforter for about a half an hour, then gave up trying to sleep. For the moment, anyway. Was she awake because she was thinking about her mother or because she couldn't get past the image of Jamie's pain, her stricken expression as she watched her mother walk away? It haunted her. She had been overwhelmed with wanting to make it go away.

She had laughed when Sheila suggested there might be something more than fragile, slightly hostile friendship between Jamie and her. Laughed because her first reaction had been, "What ever would Jamie see in me?"

She turned on her side. Jamie was serious. There was nothing superficial about her. She didn't laugh easily, and she wouldn't love easily. *I, on the other hand, do both.* In and out of love twice a year, at least before she got her nose done and took a hiatus from dating and sex. She was used to a life where you didn't put down roots because you never knew when you'd have to bug out, military style, to the next town, the next set of friends.

The Jans of the world fell in love with her. Heck, it wasn't even love. Passionate lust. Jan hadn't called since leaving. She hadn't felt the urge to call Jan, either. They gave freely of their bodies and kept their hearts intact, just like she did.

She had never suspected that she might change. Or wish she could change.

If she became rich and famous . . . What a tired refrain that was getting to be. As if that's all there is to life, she thought. But if she did, would she become another Sheila Thintowski, with conquest and sex just an extension of personal worth and personal power? Did she want to be that kind of person?

Okay, she did want to be famous. She didn't have to be rich — well, not very rich. Rich enough to keep renovating inns and houses and gardens.

Her father had had the military as the foundation of his life. It was his personal life. No matter what happened, he could fall back on the structure of the military as a safety net. Val had no such safety net. Seeing how Liesel, that funny Jacob O'Rhuan, and his sweet — for a guy — son, Jeff, had rallied around Jamie made Val realize how few of her relationships had the solidity of . . . family. Few? Try none.

160

Val, she told herself firmly, stop this. You're standing on the brink of your dreams. One thing at a time.

You have plenty of time, she whispered to her increasingly sleepy self. You're only thirty-four. Plenty of time.

# Thick Chocolate Sauce

Chocolate is not something you hurry—not eating it and not cooking with it. Patience is always rewarded when working with chocolate.

> 8 ounces (8 baker's squares) unsweetened chocolate
> (you can use chocolate chips, but try not to)
> 1 cup heavy cream at room temperature
> 1/2 cup sugar

## PREPARATION:

Chop the chocolate into smallish bits. The larger the pieces the longer the chocolate will take to melt. Chocolate chips save time but supermarket-quality chips can separate if overheated. Also, since the chips have been sweetened, the final sauce is sweeter.

## METHOD:

In double boiler, combine the sugar and 1/2 cup of the heavy cream. Stir constantly over boiling water until the mixture boils. Turn off the heat, but leave the mixture over the hot water.

Add the chocolate and stir. And stir. And stir. Do not be tempted into turning the heat back on. The chocolate will melt, eventually. If you heat the chocolate too high you risk the cocoa butter separating out.

Once the chocolate is completely melted, add the remaining cream and stir until smooth, thick, lush and decadent.

You may need to taste the finished product several times, over and over.

This sauce can be used as cake topping—it will run over the sides quite attractively. You can also fill the hole in an angel food cake with it; its semi-sweet richness is a luscious counterpoint to a sweet cake. Whatever you think would be good with chocolate probably will be!

**⊪⊪⊪⊪⊪⊪⊪ From the Waterview, Mendocino ⊪⊪⊪⊪⊪⊪⊪**

# 10

Christmas week turned wet and cold, not
unexpectedly. The fog gave way to low, black clouds
that seemed to hold oceans of rain. The covered
wooden sidewalks elevated over the street proved their
usefulness as the mud rose higher each day.

Jamie had reviewed the menu with Val for Mark
Warnell's entire proposed stay until Val could discuss
almost every aspect of the recipes comfortably. She
could also help with most of them, looking as if she
were actually in charge of their creation.

Sunday was the first day that they closed the

Waterview so they could finish the dining room floors and Jamie could concentrate on cooking for what was now a party of five: Mark Warnell, Sheila Thintowski, Graham Chester, Val and Jamie. Though Jamie was well aware that she wasn't necessarily in the party, but she had to eat, too, at least breakfast and lunch. She planned to slip out after dinner was cleared away each night to spend time with Liesel.

Liesel was combating her holiday loneliness by inviting several single friends to a midnight Christmas Eve buffet after caroling. But Jamie missed Aunt Em horribly every time she thought about it being Christmas, so she knew Liesel felt even worse. In a way, it was helpful to have so much work to do.

Today she was making the broths precisely the way Aunt Em always had. She kept the new door to the kitchen firmly closed while they sanded and varnished the floor — it would never do to get the scent of varnish into the broth.

She roasted ten pounds of beef bones, then popped them into individual stockpots. The deglazed roasting pan would contribute to the cold meat glaze. Three pots of stock would be bases for stews and soups, the remaining one for gravies and sauces. Since the weather was proving so abysmal, the arrival time of the guests was uncertain, so the lunch meal would be Italian — only the pasta had to be made at the last minute.

The racket from the dining room stopped abruptly. Having no constant stream of meals to make gave Jamie the luxury to slip out the back door and around to the front. The sidewalk was stacked with the new tables, benches and chairs. She peered between them at Val and Jeff O'Rhuan. Jeff had made himself available to do any heavy work Val needed. The two of them were moving a machine that looked like a cross between a vacuum cleaner and a sander to one end of the room. It looked really heavy.

She watched as they took much smaller machines and worked their way on their knees along the sides of the floor. Dust was everywhere. After a few minutes a piece of sandpaper flew off the bottom of Val's machine and Val got up, looking very much as if she wanted to kick the thing. She raised her goggles and Jamie burst out laughing — Val's eyes and nose were clearly outlined by a layer of fine dust.

Val heard her and sent a gesture using one finger. She turned away, so Jamie felt perfectly safe sticking out her tongue at Val's back. Geez, Val brought out primitive emotions in her.

Back in the kitchen Jamie thought idly of making chocolate cupcakes. No, she had promised herself she was through making chocolate over Val. But a little cupcake — that wasn't much. Just a little bit of chocolate.

She made the batter and turned a dozen cupcakes out in record time. Just as she finished Jacob O'Rhuan banged in the back door.

"M'darling, something smelled so good I had to stop in."

Jamie poured him a cup of coffee. "I'm warning you — this won't last as long as Liesel's."

"Liesel's coffee would revive the dead," Jacob said.

Jamie smiled to himself — Jacob could wake the dead without coffee.

"What are they doing in there?" Jacob bit into a cupcake. "Delicious, m'darling. They're making some kind of racket."

"Sanding the floors so they can be revarnished. I don't know what Val was so happy about after they stripped down the first part — something about clearcut oak."

Jacob peeled the baking paper from his second cupcake. "Floor's never been refinished as long as I've known the place. That's a long time. I wouldn't recognize it."

"I feel that way sometimes. But other times I feel as if it's mine now. Don't get me wrong —"

"I understand," Jacob assured her. "I know you loved Em like nobody, but you'll be wanting to put your own stamp on things. Em wouldn't have minded in the least."

"I didn't think she would. Because of all her hard work, my circumstances are different. No one handed her an inn free and clear as a starting-off point."

"She was a good woman." Jacob finished his third cupcake. "Liesel's been telling me you're helping Val get a big break in show business. She's a talented young gal."

"Yes, she is. Have you actually looked at the dining room lately?"

"I'm always in here, eating your goodies."

Jamie laughed. "Don't I know it, you big lug."

Jacob grinned, his beard going all bristly under the sheer energy of his good humor. "Good to have you back here, m'darling. Don't you be going away."

"I don't think I will, at least not anytime soon."

"Well, I'll go peek at my son, make sure he's not gumming up the works."

"Have a cupcake for the road," Jamie offered. "You're a growing boy."

Jacob's laugh lingered after he left, and Jamie

turned on the boom box Val had put in kitchen. She chopped crystallized fruits for *stollen*, a tasty German fruitcake. Not only would it be the first snack to welcome the weary travelers, but Jamie intended to keep her aunt's tradition of providing two dozen loaves to the church for Christmas morning service. When she was finally able to take a day off here and there she would get more involved in the church, as her aunt had been. The new pastor — only there about ten years or so — had continued its commitment as first and foremost a place where community was built and preserved. He'd been over to visit Jamie, too, mentioning in passing that prayers had been said for her aunt at services after her death. Jamie did appreciate that. Considering the method she'd chosen for her death — well, some churches might have balked.

She added cinnamon to the shopping list. All her regular suppliers had made their last deliveries before Christmas, so anything Jamie ran out of would have to come from the market. She decided she wouldn't have enough whole allspice for the mulled cider either, and added that to the list. Val had promised to go between now and Christmas Eve morning, when the guests would arrive. That was Wednesday morning — just three more days.

Stomping and scuffling at the back door heralded Val's arrival. Jamie had shut out the sanding noise so successfully she hadn't realized it had stopped.

"It's a drag going around," Val said. "Jeff is going to finish mopping the floor to get the sawdust up. But he said he'd only do it if he had one of those cupcakes his dad made a point of eating right in front of the window where we could see him."

Jamie pointed at the tin. "My fingers are gooey. Help yourself. Take Jeff some soda, too. He doesn't do coffee."

"And here I was thinking he wasn't too bad for a guy."

"He's a sweetie, just like his dad." Jamie chopped dried cranberries in sugar, then set them next to the rest of the *stollen* ingredients. "Do you like rum sauce or lemon sauce?"

"On what?"

"Fruitcake."

"I hate fruitcake."

"Not my fruitcake, you don't."

"Sure," Val said, plainly not convinced. "Lemon sauce, I guess."

"Okay, lemon sauce it is." Jamie rinsed her hands free of sugary fruit pieces. "This is the fruitcake batter, by the way. Eggs, flour, the basic sweet cake ingredients. It also has lots of nutmeg and cinnamon, molasses and brown sugar. The molasses is my aunt's touch."

"Molasses and brown sugar," Val repeated. "I'll remember that."

Jamie brushed one cutting board's contents into the batter and turned on the mixer. She lowered the beaters into the batter. Just as Jamie turned away one beater slipped out of its holder and clanked into the batter, the other beater — then the mixer made a frightening groan. Batter splattered everywhere.

"Crud!" Jamie hit the off switch, but not before she was liberally bedewed with the dark, sticky batter. It was in her hair, then dripped into one eye.

Val was laughing hysterically. Jamie sent her the same one finger gesture Val had sent earlier.

"Here, here," Val managed, between chortles. "Let me help. Come over to the sink."

Jamie leaned over the sink while Val sponged goo out of her hair. Sawdust from Val's clothes transferred to Jamie, clotting in the globs of batter. Under the sawdust was one of Val's usual T-shirts, clinging to her trim stomach and waist. Val smelled of powdery wood and lightly of deodorant. It would take only a slight movement of Jamie's head to rest against Val's hip.

The problem with fruitcake, Jamie reflected after Val had gone back to her work, was it had no chocolate. She ate the last cupcake. It didn't really help.

Val was truly nervous. The Warnell party didn't arrive until the next day, but this evening she was giving a grand tour to Jamie and Liesel, their first opportunity to see everything as a newcomer would.

All the tools were hidden, all the detritus from wallpaper, paint and stencils gone. Yesterday she'd had the nasty surprise of discovering the linens packed away by Bill were dirty and had lost several hours at a laundromat in Fort Bragg — who needed sleep, anyway? But there had been a goodly store of serviceable coverlets for each bed, their simple utilitarian lines suiting the new decor.

Her only worry was the lingering scent of varnish. She'd rented large heater fans to help dry the cold floor and combat the moisture from the unrelenting rain, but even so, the scent lingered, especially when the doors were closed. The yet-to-be-decorated

Christmas tree and the cut boughs from a second tree were putting off lots of fresh, spicy pine scent. But Val could still smell the varnish.

She lit the three fireplaces in the dining room. Directly in front of the fireplace was a family table for eight to ten people, then tables for two and four scattered around the rest of the room. The family table had a brilliant red cloth on it and a gorgeous centerpiece of holly and pine. She dimmed the lights and let the battery-powered candles in the windows and on each table provide a low, flattering glow.

"Oh my," she heard behind her.

She turned to find Liesel and Jamie standing in the doorway from the street. "Wait right there," she warned. She hurried over to the music deck and pressed play. Handel's "Lift Up Your Heads" rippled from the sound system. "Now you can come in."

Liesel's eyes were shining. "This is stunning, Val. You should be so proud. Job well done."

Jamie's eyes held a similar shine. "It looks so elegant, but I know if the lights were up it would be its normal, functional self."

"Amazing what lighting can do, isn't it?" Val pushed the dimmers all the way up and sharp lighting from hidden soffits poured down, bright as daylight. "Makes me want pie and coffee, and clam chowder in bread bowls, and celery ragout with wine." She turned off the fireplace gas and the flickering warmth quickly dissipated. "For when the sun comes out."

"It's not coming out any time soon," Liesel said. "It's going to rain through the weekend."

"Good," Val said. "That will keep Mark Warnell from wandering around asking too many questions. Come upstairs."

*  *  *  *  *

With all of the studying Val had done for the menu, Jamie wondered if there was any need for subterfuge. Well, she supposed there was. Anyone in town would tell Mark Warnell that Val had just arrived here. Jamie wasn't sure what Sheila Thintowski knew, but from the feverish way Val had finished the renovation and applied herself to cooking, it was obvious that she still felt the entire charade was necessary.

Val had no reason to be hesitant about the way the renovations had turned out, however. The guest stairway was repapered, and the creaky treads repaired. The handrails were also repainted and the new carpet runner was the same blue as the Shaker stenciling on the second floor. Val bypassed the second floor in favor of showing them the third floor, with its new "master bedroom" first.

It astonished Jamie. It was so different from the room Aunt Em had occupied for so many years. The room had been big to start with, but had no closets. Aunt Em had always used a wardrobe, which had plenty of room for her simple clothing. Val had devoted one wall to closet space, half with two sliding doors for hanging garments, and half with drawers of all sizes and a few shelves here and there. A half dozen down pillows covered the queen-size bed. The foot of the bed was draped with one of the quilts her aunt had collected.

The bathroom made Liesel sigh. "Em would have loved this. Whenever we went on vacation she would ask for a room with a bathtub."

The old Fiberglas stall shower had been replaced

with tiles and smoky glass doors. The top row of tile above the shower was stenciled with the blue and white Shaker pattern used throughout the rest of the inn. The large, clawfoot tub was big enough for two, Jamie thought, then she shied away from her mental picture of two women in particular sharing its pleasures.

It hit her then that this was going to be her home. It was lovely — she liked it very much. It also breathed Valkyrie Valentine. She would never be able to forget Val in this room.

Which was a pretty kettle of fish, she thought.

She tried not to think about it as they went through the two other bedrooms on the floor. Their common bathroom had been updated as well, with Val's decorating touches added, but otherwise they were unchanged. It wasn't hard to picture them as they had been when she and Kathy had lived there. Perhaps she should rent out the master bedroom and keep the other two rooms for herself — one for a bedroom, and one for an office and sitting room. Aunt Em had often longed for a little room of her own where she could read or pay bills in peace.

Val's belongings turned up in one of the rooms on the second floor. "I thought I would give them the upper floor . . . more privacy for us. Mark Warnell in the master, Sheila and Graham in the smaller bedrooms. So I kept my stuff in here."

"That's probably a good idea," Jamie agreed.

"Are you sure you want to go through with this?" Liesel ran a hand over a wall glazed with Wedgwood Blue before turning to Val for her answer.

Val's smile was tired. "You want me to quit, now that I've done the hard part? Not a chance, Charley."

She led the way down the widened back staircase that ended in the kitchen.

Even here there were changes, but Jamie had strictly supervised them the last two days. With the dining room closed there had been a chance to replace one of the ovens, thoroughly polish and clean the old dampers with their distinctive brass and copper workings. Bill had let them tarnish, then go black with grime. Val had worked around Jamie's head doing more stenciling on the ceiling, then replaced the facings on the cupboard doors with light maple that matched the tables and chairs in the dining room. Then, yesterday, the whole room had undergone a thick coat of clean white semi-gloss paint. To Jamie's nose it still smelled like paint, but it was getting better. A serious bout of cooking would take care of it. Serious cooking began tomorrow morning.

Liesel was hugging Val and congratulating her on how thorough she had been. "It's not a surface job — you got right into the bones of the place. She feels brand new to me. I don't see how your guests won't be impressed."

"The proof will be in Jamie's cooking, I think. They already expect this renovation at a minimum. What they don't expect is an authentic Georgian meal à la Jane Austen. It's the food that will sell them." Val turned to Jamie with a smile.

"Speaking of food," Jamie said, "I think I'll start on the chocolate leaves and bowls tonight. It can get very tedious and slow, and if they're here early I'll never get them done."

"Well, I'll see you later," Liesel said. "Though if you're too late you'll have to get your own cocoa."

Jamie grinned. "I think I can manage that."

"She gives you cocoa every night?" Val asked after Liesel had gone.

"Every night. I put my feet up and she brings me a cup of cocoa. She must have longed to do that for my aunt."

"So that Kathy creature is the reason they weren't together? I mean living together?"

Jamie nodded. "Aunt Em gave Kathy the decision. I think she hoped that Kathy would grow up a little and say it was okay. But she didn't. She said that if Liesel moved in here that everyone would know her mother was a pervert."

"Christ."

"I don't think she even realized the depth of the insult she delivered. Aunt Em was ... straight, for lack of a better word. She had said it would have to be unanimous because we all lived in the house, not just her. I mean, I'd already said I'd love it if Liesel lived with us. I loved Liesel even then. I could tell how happy Aunt Em was when Liesel was around. But Kathy said no and that was that. Aunt Em would not go back on her word."

"I don't want to speak ill of someone so well-loved, but it sounds to me like she spoiled Kathy rotten."

Jamie sighed again. "She did. And me. I just took it better. Maybe because I knew that Aunt Em didn't *have* to love me. I wasn't her kid. So I knew the gift she was giving me. I knew to cherish it. Love isn't something you take for granted." Jamie swallowed hard, wondering what had led her to give away so much to Val. She busied herself assembling ingredients; she couldn't look at Val.

Val's voice was soft. "No, you can't take it for granted. And yet some people bandy it about so easily.

174

The word, I mean. My mother sends a birthday gift every year and writes that she loves me, but I haven't seen her in at least fifteen years — her choice. I don't understand her at all."

"At least I had Aunt Em," Jamie said. "She was a mother to me, through and through."

"Oh, I had my dad. It's not like I was an orphan. Funny that we both had mothers cut from the same cloth, though."

"Funny," Jamie echoed. She set up the double boiler and turned on the big burner to get the water up to steaming.

"Well, if you're going to work, I may as well, too."

"You should get an early night. You practically haven't slept," Jamie said.

"It's early yet," Val said. "It's decadent to go to sleep before ten. I think I'll work on the ribbon-and-pine bough centerpieces — at least I can sit down while I do that. I'll be in the dining room."

Jamie carefully melted about twenty ounces of beautiful European dark chocolate, careful not to heat it so high that it separated. Once it was the right consistency, she whipped in heavy cream and butter. While it warmed she buttered sheets of kitchen parchment. Val had ordered her an extra set of stencils of the Shaker pattern, and Jamie painted them with the thickened chocolate. Then she put the trays into the walk-in refrigerator. The diamonds and leaves would look fabulous on a crystal serving dish.

She removed a tray of eight small, well-chilled bowls from the refrigerator and set about painting them with the chocolate. Chocolate bowls for chocolate mousse at dinner the day after Christmas, the last evening the Warnell party was to be with them. All in all, Jamie was glad the holiday would soon be behind them. It hadn't been much fun this year.

The only problem with the holiday being over was that Val would go away, too. Val had said there was a little more work to do — like insulating under the dining room floor. So she hadn't set a definite departure date. But she'd go.

"Damn." Her eyes were unaccountably watering, and she'd just messed up one of the bowls. It had a hole where Jamie's fingernail had caught it.

"Jamie, do you — what's wrong?"

"Nothing," Jamie said. "I just messed up a cup, and I'm happy about it."

"And you cry when you're happy."

"Right. I'm really, really happy right now."

Val stood there for a moment, then said, "Okay. But I wondered if you wanted to see the dining room with just the firelight. I think you'll love it. And then you should take off, because I'm about ready to drop and you've worked just as hard as I have."

"Let me finish this last bowl."

Val came over to inspect. "This is amazing."

"Just takes patience. Like you and the stenciling. How you can stand on a ladder for that long I'll never know."

"We make a good team," Val said.

"Complimentary skills," Jamie replied, after a swallow. "There." She lifted the tray and carried it into the refrigerator. After the chocolate had hardened a small amount of hot water swirled inside the bowl would loosen the chocolate away from the sides. It would only take a few minutes tomorrow morning.

Satisfied that the bowls were protected from damage, she followed Val into the dining room.

The new wood blinds, in the same whitewashed maple as the mantel, were closed. With just the firelight, the dining room looked like a family home. The light didn't quite reach the cash register and dessert case, and the blinds hid the new lettering and designs that Val had added to the glass.

"This is nice," Jamie said. She wandered over to the fireplace, stopping here and there to set a chair more squarely under a table. She sank down on one of the raised hearths. "These are really handy. I've been warming myself every morning right here, first thing."

"I'm glad you like it." Val sat down next to her.

Jamie found herself unaccountably nervous. Val was too close, for one thing, and in this light she looked like some kind of goddess. Even worse, Jamie was feeling a little too emotional, a little too much on the ragged edge.

"We are a good team," Val said again. When Jamie didn't answer, she said in a low voice that cut through Jamie's heart, "Jamie?"

She lifted her head to find Val leaning toward her. She couldn't turn away, she didn't want to. Val's lips were like warm silk on hers. Jamie knew she whimpered, but holding it back would have cost her the effort she was making to keep from throwing herself into Val's arms.

The kiss was long, long enough to make the fire at Jamie's back seem cool by comparison. Her heart was hammering in her ears and nothing seemed real except for the press of Val's lips.

Then Val opened her mouth with a deep sigh that Jamie was helpless to resist. She responded with a gasp and tasted Val's mouth on hers, all the while holding her hands rigidly at her sides, unwilling to take the consequences of what would happen if she touched Val and her restraint gave way to the flood of long-banked need.

When Val's fingertips brushed her cheeks, the sensation was so sweet, and so welcome, that she panicked. Val lurched into the space where Jamie had been as Jamie dashed toward the kitchen, saying breathlessly, "I forgot to close the refrigerator."

Val was following her. Jamie dashed through the kitchen to the walk-in refrigerator, opened the door and pulled it shut behind her. Silly, she thought, Val knows how to open the door.

Open it she did. She was framed in the kitchen light like a primordial being, glowing with energy and power.

The primordial being said, "Are you nuts?"

"No, I just didn't want to ruin the chocolate." Jamie brushed her fingers lightly over the fully set chocolate stencils.

"Then I'll just close the door," Val said. She did. But she was on the inside.

Jamie backed into the corner.

"I'm not going to hurt you," Val said. "What on earth do you think I have in mind? I just wanted . . . to kiss you. Because we make a good team."

"I'm not interested in that kind of partnership."

"Fine," Val said. "A kiss is just a kiss."

Maybe to you, Jamie wanted to say. Instead she said, "Like with Jan?"

"Jealous?"

"Of course not."

Val was taking slow steps toward Jamie. "You're going to freeze in here."

"I'm fine. I'm used to it."

"Jamie, come out into the kitchen." She reached for Jamie's hand.

"No."

"Jamie . . ." Val took her hand. It was electrically hot against Jamie's rapidly chilling fingers. "I'm sorry I frightened you. It was the last thought on my mind."

"I'm not frightened." Jamie trembled. "I'm cold."

"Come into the kitchen," Val repeated.

"I've got work to do."

"Christ, Jamie. So do I." Val's voice cracked and her brilliant blue eyes flashed. "I have things I need to do. Like this."

Her mouth found Jamie's again, this time more firmly. Jamie's knees, against all laws of physics, melted. Val held her pinned against the chilled boxes of cheese and milk. Her warm arms went around Jamie, and Jamie thought she would faint.

She kissed Val back. She wrapped her arms around Val's waist and returned the kiss, pressure for pressure, taste for taste.

When Val drew back, she whispered against Jamie's eyes, "Was that so bad?"

"No," Jamie admitted. "A kiss is just a kiss."

Val sighed, not passionately this time, and she let Jamie go. "We'll catch our death if we stay in here much longer."

"Right," Jamie said.

Val opened the door and Jamie turned off the light. In the kitchen, Jamie fussed around the leftover chocolate in the double boiler. It was still warm and semi-soft.

"I wonder what I could use this up on?"

Val came over to examine it. "Would it make chocolate milk?"

"Wouldn't dissolve. You'd have chocolate pellets in white milk."

"Frosting?"

"Hmm, it would be a soft dip for cupcakes if we had any left."

"Well," Val said, "we could eat it with our fingers."

Jamie started to tremble again. She scooped up some of the soft, slightly runny chocolate on her index finger and offered it to Val.

Val slowly and deliberately took Jamie's finger in her mouth, licking the chocolate away. Her tongue lingered longer than necessary and Jamie knew that Val must feel her quivering.

Val reached for the bowl of chocolate, but Jamie said, her voice barely audible, "Let me." She offered more chocolate to Val, but as Val drew close to accept it, Jamie swept it across Val's mouth and cheek. "We could paint with it."

Val made a low sound that Jamie echoed as their mouths met, hungry for each other and tasting chocolate and passion with every movement of their tongues. They parted, gasping, and Jamie felt Val's chocolate-dipped fingers on her face, then they were smoothing across her throat. Then those fingers found their way under her apron, to her shirt buttons.

Jamie eased Val's T-shirt out of her jeans, fumbled for the bowl, then painted a long stripe of chocolate down Val's spine. The T-shirt cleared Val's head just as Val pulled Jamie's shirt away. There was a moment's frustration when the apron tangled, then

Val undid it all, including Jamie's bra, and tugged everything away.

Jamie swayed on her feet. Val's hands were coated with warm chocolate as she molded Jamie's breasts, her tongue following her hands.

Jamie painted the back of Val's neck, aware that she was losing control of her desires, would lose control of her better sense if this went on. But how could she stop? Val's hands and mouth were at her zipper, and within a few heartbeats she was naked, covered with chocolate, in her own kitchen, and open to anything Val wanted to do to her.

Val was slowly sinking to her knees. She pushed Jamie back against the counter and used the last of the chocolate on her hands to paint the insides of Jamie's thighs. She eased Jamie's legs apart and Jamie gasped for air. The room was spinning.

All that held her to the planet was Val's mouth searching everywhere Jamie so badly needed her.

"There," she gasped.

Val pressed her mouth to Jamie so hard she realized her feet were barely on the floor. Jamie grabbed a cabinet handle, prayed Val had bolted it on tight and coiled herself for an explosion — she was going to explode.

She didn't explode physically, but mentally she crashed into a dozen different pieces. Ecstasy ripped through her body as Val groaned and pulled Jamie's legs onto her shoulders. She groaned again as the pent up longing of too many years brought Jamie to a shuddering climax, punctuated by a cry of release.

Then Val was standing up, pulling the naked Jamie against her half-naked body. They kissed, forever mixing the smell of sex and the scent of chocolate in Jamie's mind. Her hands fumbled with Val's bra, and then they were on the floor, Val's torso smeared with chocolate and the print of Jamie's breasts. Jamie cried out again as her fingertips entered Val — she'd forgotten, oh, she'd forgotten. Such softness and such wetness, then the clench of muscles unbelievably strong. She pushed against them and Val clutched Jamie's mouth to her breasts, straining.

There was chocolate and sex everywhere. When Val suggested they take a shower there was nothing else to do but agree. From the shower they went to Val's bed. Jamie fell into Val's passion, and let it roll her over to new sense of life, a new sense of being alive.

The scent of chocolate lingered in Val's hair.

## Mulled Cider

This is so easy, trust me. Pick your most attractive kettle or pot or even an old percolater (remember those?). If you use a percolater clean the inside by perking a packet of KoolAid and water through it, then rinsing. Whatever you use to mull the cider will be on your stovetop or buffet table, so pick something nice to look at.

Get a big jug of apple cider, a small can of orange juice concentrate, stick cinnamon (at least 6 sticks) and whole allspice. (If you're going to use a percolater, use ground cinnamon and ground allspice.) Put the cider, 6 sticks of cinnamon (or 1 tablespoon ground) and 2 teaspoons of allspice pods (or 1/2 teaspoon ground) and 1/2 of the orange juice concentrate in the pot and bring to a slow boil or perk it through one cycle. Let it simmer for a while. Taste.

If you want more of any spice, add it. More citrus? Add more orange juice. Be careful with the allspice, though, it can get bitter. If it gets bitter, add some sugar. Some people also like nutmeg.

Keep it hot. Serve in any kind of hot cup, from cut crystal punch glasses to your matching Star Trek mugs—it's your house and your party. Only cry if you want to.

# 11

The bed was shaking. Jamie stirred and then realized where she was.

Val sneezed again, then swore.

Jamie opened one eye. The light was pre-dawn, but not by much. She glanced at Val, then sat bolt upright, alarmed to see Val holding a red splotched washcloth to her nose.

"Damn sneezing," Val snuffled. "Sets off my sinuses."

"Do you get allergy attacks often?"

"Not allergies. Bad sinuses. All plastic surgeons should be shot."

"Plastic surgeons," Jamie echoed, feeling stupid. "Good morning, by the way."

Val smiled softly. "Good morning to you. I'd kiss you but . . ."

"Please don't. Why should plastic surgeons be shot?"

"Because they didn't tell me that my sinuses would remain irritated and fragile more than six months after surgery."

Val had had plastic surgery? Was that why she had such incredible cheekbones, those full lips? Were her eyes really that color, or was it just tinted lenses? And those breasts — how much of their magnificence was due to a surgeon's expertise? She must very badly want to be a star.

Jamie began to feel as if she'd spent the night with Barbie. She also began to realize the enormity of what she'd done. Val could hardly be in any doubt of Jamie's feelings now.

"Why did you have plastic surgery?"

"I had a big nose." Val sniffed. "I think it's letting up. I hate nosebleeds."

"How big?"

"You heard of Pinocchio?"

"Oh."

"You don't approve."

"It's not for me to say."

"But you don't approve. At least give me the courtesy of being honest."

That stung. "It just seems that if Barbra Streisand can live with a big nose, so can you."

Val's eyes flashed. "Big nose? *Big nose*? Streisand's

nose looks like a button compared to the nose I had. And what the hell is it to you anyway?"

"Nothing at all."

"But?"

"But nothing."

"But you think people should live with what they're dealt. That cosmetic surgery is vain."

"I didn't say that."

"You're thinking it."

"You're projecting."

"No, I'm not. I finally found the guts to have my nose cut off. I did it because the face in the mirror didn't match who I thought I was. It's not like I'm Kathryn Hellman in Brazil. I could have capped my teeth and taken care of this scar on my eyebrow and ordered tinted lenses and had my ears tucked, my tummy tucked, my lower lip zapped with collagen. All it takes is money. But all I did was lop off the extra cartilage on my nose."

"Sounds like you're still justifying it to yourself." Jamie just barely kept herself from adding that Val's eyes were already blue-green enough and her lower lip one of the most intriguing features of her face. She could not admit that Val's lower lip, and upper lip for that matter, caused her endless consternation.

Instead she threw her legs over the side of the bed. "I have to go home and change. We have guests and a lot of work to do before they get here."

"Jamie —"

"Liesel must be worried sick." Jamie flushed when she realized she was looking for clothes that were still in the kitchen. "I'll just head down for my clothes and let myself out."

"Jamie —"

"I'll put your clothes on the stairs." Good lord, what if someone had come in and found their bras and underwear smeared with chocolate. Jamie felt slightly ill.

"Jamie —"

"See you later."

"Jamie, goddammit! Talk to me."

"About what?" She paused with her hand on the knob.

"Didn't last night mean anything to you?"

It had meant the world. It was breaking Jamie's heart. Val was leaving — it would do her well to remember that from now on. "A kiss is just a kiss, right?" She could not look at Val.

After a moment, Val said, "Yeah, right."

"Okay."

"Fine."

"See you later."

"Great."

Jamie crept down the stairs, relieved to see there were no lights on downstairs. She scampered into her clothes and headed out the door.

Liesel was already making coffee. "Jamie, you startled me. I thought you were in your room."

"No, I, uh —"

"You haven't worked all night have you? You need your sleep."

"Not precisely." She took off her jacket and then realized Liesel was staring at her shirt. She glanced down.

Val's palm print in chocolate was plainly visible right over her breast.

"What precisely, then? Wait — forget I asked. I'm not Em. You don't have to account for your time with me." Liesel went back to cracking eggs.

"We spent the night together," Jamie said.

"Was that wise, *liebchen*?"

"No." Jamie's ragged composure cracked clean down the middle, and she cried like she hadn't cried since Kathy had told her to leave her alone. This was different . . . that had been a bad case of puppy love. A bad case of wanting life to be perfect. This was deeper, more mature.

But just as wasted.

Liesel's gentle pats and hugs helped Jamie get past the tears, but they didn't help the ache inside. Liesel plied her with food, then sent her for a very hot shower.

Jamie let the steam soak into her and wondered what to do. She had no choice but to go back and help Val for the next few days. She had made a bargain and, given the beautiful work Val had done, no doubt she'd gotten the best of it. Unless you counted the broken heart.

Going back was going to be one of the hardest things she'd ever done.

She drank two cups of Liesel's coffee but still felt foggy. So caffeine wasn't helping, and eating any form of chocolate was right out. She'd make herself a bowl of noodles with butter, first chance she got. When coffee and chocolate didn't work, pasta was the next thing to try.

After pasta came bread, then a thick steak, and then fresh-squeezed fruit juices. It could take days, months even, before she found the cure for Val. But a cure would be found, even if it took her the rest of her life.


Val wanted to walk up to Jamie and say, "Jamie, I don't get you."

They had had the single most passionate night of Val's life. And that was saying something. Yet Jamie acted as if it hadn't even left her with a raised temperature. She stood there in front of the very stove where chocolate had softened, standing on the spot where she'd taken Val. Val felt faint just remembering the way Jamie had leaned over her.

"I think it's going to rain all day," Val finally said. Right, talk about the weather instead of saying how much you want her.

"Probably. This is a good northern coast downpour."

"Do you need any help?"

"No, I'm fine. Just remember when they get here to bring them to the kitchen to chat while you heat up the lemon sauce." Jamie tapped a small saucepan. "I'll make myself scarce at first. And offer coffee."

"Like, duh."

Jamie flicked an impatient glance at her. "Do you want my help?"

"Of course." *I want you. I want your help for a very long time. Like maybe forever.*

"Then just try to remember what I'm telling you."

Val couldn't help herself. "Someone got up on the wrong side of my bed this morning."

"Does it happen often?"

Ouch. "That really wasn't necessary."

190

"Jan's been gone two weeks and you couldn't leave me alone."

"Oh, so I seduced you?"

"Who started kissing who?"

"Who suggested painting each other with chocolate?"

Jamie blushed. Well, at least she seemed to remember that. "After you . . ."

"After I what? Oh, forget it. Just forget it." Val stormed upstairs to change into a pair of gray linen slacks and a tight-fitting white silk shirt with large, romantically poetic sleeves. She didn't say a word as she put on a snowy white apron in the kitchen, then went into the dining room to fuss with the Christmas tree.

About ten minutes later she saw a large car pull up in front of the inn. She caught a glimpse of Sheila Thintowski in the back seat. She forgot she was mad at Jamie. "They're here," she called in a cracking voice.

"Remember the lemon sauce," Jamie called back. "I'll be back, just arriving to work."

Val met the party at the door. Sheila was in the lead, shaking her umbrella. Val kissed her and welcomed her, then turned her attention to the two men. She saw a driver scrambling to get luggage out of the trunk of the car.

"Miss Valentine, it's a pleasure to meet one of my writers." Val shook hands with the man who must be Graham Chester. "I don't want to put pressure on you, but I love Christmas in New York, and this isn't New York."

"I'll hope to make it up to you, Mr. Chester," Val said solemnly. Gay, gayer and gayest, she thought. Her gaydar had been pretty accurate lately. She turned to the other man. "You must be Mr. Warnell."

He shook her hand forcefully. He was much younger than she had expected, and more . . . virile. He exuded masculinity. She imagined that a great many women, as well as a few men, fell prey to that charm. Graham Chester perhaps?

"It's certainly a pleasure, Ms. Valentine. You and your inn are every bit as spectacular as I was led to believe."

"Thank you," Val said. What else do you say to a compliment that extravagant? "You have to call me Val, though. I insist."

Both men insisted she call them by first name, then Val took their coats and directed the driver with the first load of luggage up to the third floor. He gave her a pained look and headed up the stairs.

"You must be frozen — the weather is awful. Come into the kitchen and I'll warm up something to tide us over to lunch."

"We were famished after getting up so early," Sheila said as they moved toward the kitchen. "So we grabbed something . . . well, it wasn't precisely food, in Fort Bragg."

"Then we'll make lunch a light, but memorable meal. Fort Bragg is not noted for its cuisine. Though there are a few excellent restaurants there."

She continued to chatter with a facility that frightened her. She hadn't realized she could be so vapid. She managed to keep it up all the while the lemon sauce heated, then she tried to look carefree as she sliced the *stollen* according to Jamie's instructions — stollen took four passes of the knife because of the nuts — and put the slices on plates. Within a few minutes everyone had warm fruitcake drizzled with lemon sauce and steaming mugs of mulled cider punch.

Mark Warnell made no bones about liking the stollen. He licked his fork with satisfaction. Val decided that this man was an accidental jet setter. He wasn't uncouth, just unpretentious.

The driver clunked down the back stairs and looked longingly at the coffee and cake, so Val did what Jamie would have done, served him a slice and poured a large cup of coffee.

"You've earned it," she said. "The drive must have been terrible."

"It wasn't great," Sheila said. "We were going to have Len return to San Francisco today and drive back for us on Saturday, but given the weather, I don't suppose . . ."

"We've got lots of room and lots of food if Len can miss Christmas at home."

"It'd be great to stay," Len said with a shy smile.

"Welcome to Waterview, then."

He ducked his head, then glanced at Graham Chester. Definitely a San Francisco fellow, Val thought. Well, the inn had been inaugurated by one night of homosexual passion. Graham and Len could have all the fun they wanted as long as they didn't wear spurs to bed.

"Sheila tells me you've been rushing some renovations."

"I couldn't wait until after you'd visited. I wanted everything to be right."

"Well, it's beautiful, so far. I'm impressed."

Val saw Sheila visibly relax. She relaxed, too, so she said with more confidence than she thought possible, "Wait until Christmas dinner. You ain't seen nothing yet."

At that moment the back door opened and Jamie came in, looking as if she was just arriving for the day.

She introduced Jamie as the chef's assistant, then put her to work preparing the lunch that Jamie had already half made. Jamie was meek, and when she worked on the herbs her knife was silent, not the usual rapid-fire chopping Val was used to.

They took a tour of the inn and Val felt very comfortable discussing the work that had been done. After all, she'd done it. With Jamie's rehearsing the menu points with her, she also felt at ease discussing the cold meat dinner planned for the evening. The rain might put a nix on caroling.

That was when she found out Graham Chester was a vegetarian. She shot a look at Sheila — Sheila might have warned her. No doubt Jamie would know what to do, but she hadn't a clue.

"There are plenty of vegetables and more than enough interesting sauces. And we're having a light Italian feast for lunch."

"Pasta and I are old friends," Graham said. "I do eat seafood."

Val crossed her fingers that she had really seen salmon in the refrigerator. "I think we can manage a poached salmon filet for dinner then."

"A flexible cook," Mark boomed. "That's amazing. I can't wait to try everything."

After a luncheon of delectable grilled garlic toast, gnocchi noodles with shrimp and tomatoes, and raspberry lemon ice for dessert, Mark Warnell insisted on seeing the town. The rain did not deter him.

\* \* \* \* \*

The last Jamie saw of the party for the afternoon was Val's worried face going out the front door.

But the less she saw of Val the better. She wanted to get through her cooking and serving, then get the hell away from Val and her scheme. That it would work was in no doubt. That she would survive the next two days was another question entirely.

A cold menu for dinner meant she could do almost everything ahead of time. Cold poached salmon replaced chicken and would suit Graham Chester's taste. Tomorrow's dinner was another thing. Certainly there were numerous vegetarian dishes planned, but the main course was pheasant. What could she make for Graham's main course? More salmon? Two days in a row wasn't particularly appetizing.

She left the dinner dishes assembled and ready, then wrote a note to Val saying she was "on break." She took a quick walk to Jacob O'Rhuan's to see what he had in the freezer.

"M'darling, anything for you," was Jacob's answer when Jamie explained her dilemma.

"I knew you'd have something good, and the stores are all closed by now."

"I've got nothing fresh, just by way of warning. Water's too churned up for anything. But I froze this halibut a month ago. Out of the water maybe five hours before I did it."

Jacob used a commercial vacuum sealer after he gutted fish. The halibut eye was clear and she knew that Jacob gutted fish properly. "This will be great. It's not too big."

"I also have some mahi-mahi. Very fancy." Jacob scrabbled in his deep freeze.

"From these waters?"

"Oh no, lass. I traded a fresh Pacific salmon over-night mail with a fellow I know in Hawaii. We do that a couple times a year. Nothing like it fresh."

"I can't take your mahi-mahi."

"M'darling, you can have anything I've got. Em would reach right down from heaven and smack me if I didn't help out."

Jamie pulled Jacob's beard, just as if she were still twelve. "You big lug."

The rain was letting up a little as she trudged up the hill toward the inn. Her slicker let her pass the Warnell party in complete anonymity as they came out of Mendocino Jams & Jellies. She took unreasonably spiteful pleasure in the inadequacy of Sheila Thintowski's umbrella and short jacket. She was getting soaked. Val wasn't faring much better.

The fish went into the smaller refrigerator to thaw and Jamie finished making the salad dressing, which was Aunt Em's secret recipe for Thousand Island dressing. It was perfect for a raw vegetable dip, and with more chilies, it made a spicy topping for cold fish. She hoped that Graham Chester liked it.

When the party came back everyone retired to their rooms to find dry clothing. The next convening would be for dinner.

Jamie tried very hard not to feel a knot in her stomach when Val reappeared a short time later. She did not take any notice of the forest-green sweater over black linen slacks that highlighted Val's shoulders and waist. She did not peek through the pass-through when Val went to the dining room to fuss over the table and set the lighting to her liking.

Sheila Thintowski appeared next, in a little black dress like something Audrey Hepburn wore in *Breakfast at Tiffany's*. She used the back stairs and startled Jamie.

"What exactly is Val making for dinner?"

Jamie raised her voice so Val would hear. "I think it's cold meat and salad with a hot soup to start and hot cobbler after."

She saw Val glance toward the kitchen, then head in their direction.

"Sheila, you changed quick. Didn't you want a hot shower? My feet were half-frozen." Val put on an apron and got several spoons out of the drawer.

"I didn't want to miss a moment with you," Sheila said. She lowered her eyelashes, all flirt.

Oh, puh-leaze, Jamie thought.

Val went into the prearranged script she and Jamie had created. "Well, I've got some arranging to do for dinner and several different things to taste and approve —"

"Let me taste, too. It'll be fun."

Val hesitated, then got out more spoons.

Since Val didn't know about the salmon or the dressing, Jamie said, "I've got your Island dressing made — the recipe was really easy to follow. And the salmon is poached. Do you want me to put the lemon in a seed bag?" Her eyes telegraphed to Val that the correct answer was yes.

If Val had no idea what a seed bag was, it didn't

show. "Of course." She tasted the dressing and then invited Sheila to do the same. Both women approved and Val tossed her spoon in the sink.

Sheila laughed and tossed hers in as well. Jamie cut a lemon in half and wrapped it in a small square of cheesecloth to catch seeds if Graham squeezed it on his fish. She tied it with a short length of ribbon.

"You're learning," Val said. "And the plates you did look really great." She went about completing three more dinner plates to match the ones Jamie had done, looking all the while like the mastermind of the entire menu.

This will work, Jamie thought. And after it did Val would get on her rocket and ride out of town. So be it.

The kitchen was a little crowded when everyone, including Len, gathered to chat and eyeball the assembling of the meal.

Graham Chester had both eyes on Len as he talked to Jamie about Mendocino and how long she'd lived there, the local economy and similar topics. He was easy to talk to, and Jamie relaxed. That is, she relaxed until she realized that Graham was not watching Len anymore, he was watching her chop celery without even looking at her hands, her knife beating like castanets on the cutting board.

Everyone had stopped talking, then Jamie recalled that she was not supposed to have such a refined cutting skill. Her hand faltered and she felt a blush rising.

Val saved her. "Jamie, you've been practicing."

"Just like you showed me," Jamie answered with only the slightest of quivers.

Graham Chester looked intrigued, then Len moved and his eyes returned to watching the driver.

"Well, I meant for this to be a little more formal, but heck," Val said. "It's Christmas Eve and many hands make light work. Everybody grab a plate. Graham, this is yours, and Jamie will bring the soup."

"I feel like I'm at home," Mark told Val as they all tromped into the dining room. "I'm not much for ceremony."

"Tell that to the genuflecting M.B.A.s at the office," Sheila said.

"They figure it out sooner or later. You did."

"The firelight is wonderful," Graham said to Jamie. "Is that something Val added?"

"It was all her idea," Jamie said honestly.

"Nice."

Val was saying to Mark, "This meal is along the lines of a Regency Era picnic. But we're having hot soup and dessert to keep the chill away."

"Tell me about all the dishes." Mark's genuine interest softened the command.

Val waited until everyone was settled before she began. "Everyone except Graham is having sliced lamb and beef with gravy. The English gravy at the time was more of a glaze than something you'd dunk a biscuit into. The salad is watercress, broccoli and asparagus with some other herbs. Macaroni with *Parmigiano Reggiano* and butter. The soup is a traditional creamed onion."

Jamie ladled soup and then fetched the basket of hot rolls she'd forgotten.

"After dinner we can join the caroling and get all wet again."

"Let's not," Sheila said quickly.

"It'll be fun," Mark said. "We used to carol when I was a kid. I haven't done any singing since I was in college."

Sheila glanced down at her attire and sighed.

"I have several slickers and sets of rainboots that are available to be borrowed," Jamie said without thinking. She recovered with, "I'm always wearing them here and then not wearing them home." Drat — she should have said that *Val* had the emergency supply on the wet porch.

This was getting tedious.

As Val dished up the cobbler, Mark complimented her on the meal. "I never realized that cold meat could be so moist. That glaze really adds something."

"I'm sure it's full of fat, just what your arteries need," Sheila said.

"The gravy broth was thoroughly skimmed of fat," Jamie said, again without thinking. Val looked at her wild-eyed. "I watched Val do it myself."

"The salmon was superb. I pity you meat-eaters." Graham leaned over to look at the steaming cobbler. "Now, what makes a cobbler a cobbler?"

Val said quickly, "I need a different spoon," and headed for the kitchen.

Jamie filled in. "Val told me that a cobbler is a very old dish in many cultures. It's fruit in season or canned covered with sweetened topping. In this case, Val used coconut, brown sugar cut with flour, and a whole lot of butter. I'm pretty sure that it is *not* fat free."

Mark said, "This holiday I am not worrying about fat."

Val returned with a different spoon and a bowl of whipped cream and resumed serving. "The trick to a good cobbler is how you masturbate the fruit with sugar."

There was a stunned silence, then Graham said very drolly, "I beg your pardon?"

Mark guffawed. "Is that a Freudian slip?"

Val crimsoned. "I was thinking about too many things at once. Of course I meant macerate."

Sheila leaned forward with a coy look. "Of course you were. Very Freudian."

"Stop that nonsense right away," Val said with mock severity. "Stop or I shall have to summon a policeman."

"Let's just hope you don't Freudian slip on camera," Mark said.

Val's eyes widened. "Implying that —"

"Let's not talk business," Mark said. "Let's save it all for the day after Christmas. We'll have a lot to iron out."

Val's eyes glowed and Jamie knew then that she had lost her. Val was going to be famous and that was that.

When there was a knock at the door she was just as pleased. The cobbler tasted of sawdust to her. "I'll get it." She wondered who would be knocking at this hour on Christmas Eve. The Closed sign was very much in evidence.

She nodded in surprise to the County Sheriff, Norm Peterson. He'd been a regular of Aunt Em's and had recently begun eating at the Waterview again.

"Real sorry about this, Jamie. I've got a court order for you to stop all business, and show cause why the inn should not be considered a part of Em's estate belonging to her daughter."

Kathy stepped out of the dark. "Thanks for the renovation. But now it's mine."

Jamie stared at them both. She blinked and shook her head, but they were still there.

# Three Easy Sauces for Crudité

Crudité (crew-dih-tay) is one of those fancy words for something simple: cut, raw vegetables. If you have the time and equipment you can do something interesting: waffled carrots, cherry tomato roses, etc. Otherwise, wash vegetables carefully in cold water, then cut them into comfortable bite-size chunks. Be sure to get a variety of colors to make a bright display. Chopped egg whites can be useful to break up too many greens. If you stack a different layer of vegetables (plus cooked meat if you like) around a bowl inverted on a platter until the bowl is hidden, you have made Salmagundy, a favorite party display that dates back to Jane Austen's era.

These vegetables will stay crisp if well-chilled before serving: Jicama, Green and Red Peppers, Gherkins, Broccoli, Radishes, Carrots, Celery sticks, Zucchini, Cucumber, Walla Walla onions. Keep Radishes away from the white vegetables or egg white—they'll stain the white red.

## Curried Mayonnaise

1/2 tbsp. hot or mild curry powder
1/2 tsp. turmeric
1-1/2 cups mayo or nonfat yogurt
In a little fying pan, shake the curry powder and turmeric over medium heat until fragrant, but not burnt. Let cool, then stir into the mayo until completely incorporated. Add 2-4 tablespoons any flavor chutney, if you have it.

## Family Secret Sauce

1/4 cup yellow mustard
1/3 cup ketchup
Stir Thoroughly
(that was easy, wasn't it?
good on burgers &
hot dogs, too)

## Island Dressing

1 cup mayonnaise
1/3 cup cocktail sauce
1/2 tsp. paprika
Tabasco™, if you like it
whisk until very smooth; taste and consider adding 1 tbsp. chopped pimiento and 1 tbsp. pickle relish

# 12

Norm grunted. "Don't be so hasty. It's not yours yet. Jamie, all I need from you is your business license and your agreement to stop operating the business until you can appear in court. Date's set for next Tuesday."

"I'm entertaining friends for the next couple of days, not running the dining room. And I've got no boarders," Jamie said. She was livid, but a rigid calm held it in check. She simply could not believe this was happening. "She had a will, Norm. She left it all to me."

"I believe you —"

"Now wait a minute," Kathy said. "You're supposed to enforce that order."

"I am, ma'am."

Norm was plenty angry himself, Jamie could tell. He never called anyone ma'am.

"Jamie, what's going on?" Val peered over Jamie's shoulder, stiffening at the sight of a policeman. "Good lord, I was just kidding."

"Kathy's trying to take the inn away from me."

"Val, is there some sort of problem?" Mark Warnell hadn't gotten up from the table, but Jamie knew he would in a moment or two.

"No, nothing at all. Just a little local business," Val said.

Kathy suddenly stepped forward, craning her neck to see who was in the dining room.

Jamie stepped in her way. "You're not setting foot in here. I reserve the right to refuse service to anyone."

Norm said, "I really don't want any trouble. It's Christmas Eve."

Val whispered intently, "We're entertaining friends. Could we perhaps discuss this further in the kitchen? Could you meet us round the back, please?"

"Sure," Norm said. He gestured firmly at Kathy to precede him.

Val was pale. "I knew everything was going too well."

"Coffee and pie isn't going to fix this," Jamie said. She felt numb and enraged at the same time.

"We'll be right back," Val said to the others. "Just a little discussion to complete." She pulled Jamie toward the kitchen.

Norm came in, shaking off rain. Kathy followed, looking sullen and satisfied at the same time.

"All I need is your license, Jamie, and I'll be heading home to my family." He glared meaningfully at Kathy.

"Make her stop serving now," Kathy said. "I'm sure she's getting paid for this."

"I am not. They're my guests."

"In the inn that should have been mine," Kathy retorted. "I don't know how you convinced my mother to leave you all her money."

"I didn't convince her of anything, you . . . you . . . brat!"

Val said, "Bravo, Jamie."

"Shut up, Val," Jamie snapped.

"Is this your new girlfriend," Kathy asked with a sneer. "She even looks a little bit like mother."

Jamie gasped. "What's that supposed to mean?"

Kathy adopted an all-knowing attitude. She addressed herself to Norm, who looked as if he wanted to be anywhere but there. "The only reason she tried to seduce me was because she couldn't seduce my mother."

"That's not true," Jamie hissed.

"Oh, get over it," Kathy said. "You were in love with her."

Jamie was glad there were no kitchen knives in reach.

"We all loved Em," Norm said. "A fine woman." When Kathy would have interrupted him, he added, "This doesn't serve any point. It's best we leave now."

Kathy burbled an incoherent protest, drowned out by Jamie's "Good God, Kathy. Are you so down on yourself that you couldn't believe I loved you for you?"

"Val, what exactly is going on?" They all turned to see Sheila entering the kitchen. Sheila assessed the situation and turned to Val. "Want to take it from the top?"

Jamie fumbled to get her framed business license from the drawer where they'd stashed it for the Warnell visit. She wanted Kathy out of her inn. She'd fight Kathy to the bitter end, too.

"This deal going through means a lot to you, right?" Val put her mouth close to Sheila's ear to avoid being overheard.

"Yes," Sheila answered.

"Then don't ask questions. The birdwoman over there is trying to shut us down. She and Jamie had a thing once upon a time and now that she's decided she's straight she's out to make sure Jamie gets run out of town."

"If she's straight then I'm Greta Garbo," Sheila said.

"If we don't get her out of here, I'm not kidding, everything is going to fall apart. Mark Warnell is going to find out that Jamie owns this place, not me."

Sheila gaped. "How could you do this to me?"

"Do what? Warnell loves the place and the cooking. The deal's in the bag — but that woman has got to go, now."

"You don't understand. If he finds out, I'll never get a chance to do another project. I presented him with a complete background check, and missed this entire mess. Daddy hates sloppy work."

"Daddy?"

Sheila whispered vehemently, "Fuck you, Val. You might have warned me." Her anger then seemed to melt away. "But you're right, the deal's in the bag. Business is business, even if you have lied to me, big time. I can't do anything about that. Besides, I'm going to love proving to this creature that she can't pass for straight. I hate that. Do you think I can do it?"

"Sheila, I think you could get Anita Bryant into bed."

Sheila actually smiled. "Everybody loves me, baby — what's the matter with you?"

Val decided that honesty was finally the best policy. "Spoken for."

"I had a feeling." Sheila turned her most sympathetic smile onto Kathy as she stepped away from Val. "I don't come from around here so I don't know what the problem is —"

"The problem is that this nobody used her perverted influence to get my mother to leave her all her money."

"How awful," Sheila said. She put her arm around Kathy. "How terribly awful for you. Do you have a headache? You look like I do when I'm having a migraine."

Kathy was eating up Sheila's sympathy with a spoon. "I do have a dreadful headache."

"I've done my job here," Norm said. He gestured with Jamie's business license. "Hope I can give this back to you soon."

"Me, too, Norm. Merry Christmas to Marge and the kids."

"I've got a wonderful prescription for headaches upstairs," Sheila was saying. Val could tell Sheila was unleashing her high voltage pheromones. "Why don't you come upstairs and take a tablet? I'm pretty good at massage too. I'll have you feeling like a million bucks."

Val wasn't surprised when Kathy went along with Sheila, pouring her tale of woe in Sheila's willing ear. She was certain that Sheila's hand gliding across Kathy's back had something to do with it. Sheila obviously liked a challenge.

"Everything settled?" Mark Warnell was busy packing a pipe when Val returned.

"Yes," Val said. "Sheila offered to help someone who stopped in. She might be back down later."

"She didn't want to go caroling anyway," Mark said. "She's not that kind of girl."

"Neither am I," Graham said.

Mark snorted.

"You know what I mean. I'm going to be perfectly content to sit here and be warm by the fire."

Val heard a refrain of "Jingle Bells" from down the street. "Jamie will clear up, so why don't we go? What about you, Len?"

"I think I'll stay by the fire myself," Len said. Of course he would, Val thought.

Val offered Mark a slicker and boots and draped herself in them as well. Jamie was nowhere in sight. Feeling as if she were in a Dali painting, Val let Mark Warnell tuck her hand under his arm, and they stepped out into the rain to sing "Jingle Bells."

\* \* \* \* \*

This was a nightmare. Jamie sat in one of the empty guest rooms holding the court order in her numb hands. She heard the carolers but couldn't join them — her head was spinning.

After a while she heard footsteps leading to the third floor. She had no idea who was where. It sounded like whoever it was had Kathy's old room.

She shut the footsteps out of her mind, so it was a while before she realized the bed overhead was squeaking rhythmically. Good God.

She heard a woman's voice rising — Sheila's. Sheila was with somebody, and the only other woman in the place was Val.

Damn it all.

Jamie stormed down to the kitchen and just barely kept herself from throwing all the preparations for tomorrow's dinner down the drain. She did the dishes in a foul mood, raging at Kathy for her selfishness, Val for her round heels, and Sheila Thintowski for being the one Val turned to after Jamie. Everyone got to have fun and she was up to her elbows in suds. Her mood was so foul she hoped she didn't ruin Liesel's gathering later.

She finished the dishes in record time, started the dishwasher and stalked out of the inn. She hoped the slamming door startled the lovebirds.


Val had set her alarm clock early, but Jamie was still in the kitchen ahead of her. Christmas morning breakfast was Belgian waffles with freshly stewed apples and lots of melted butter. Jamie looked tired, which surprised Val. She'd already left by the time she and Mark returned from caroling, and that hadn't been late.

If anyone should have bags under her eyes, it was her. Just as Graham and Len shut up, Sheila and Kathy had revved up. It had been a noisy night. She should have packed the walls with insulation.

She put a small wrapped package in front of Jamie. "Merry Christmas."

Jamie continued coring apples. "You're up early."

"Lots to do. "

"Sorry I bugged out last night. I had a lot on my mind. Oh, and I want to go over for the church service later."

"Of course. Aren't you going to open your present?"

Val got the impression that Jamie wanted to refuse, then she put down the apple and knife and rinsed her hands.

"I didn't get you anything."

"That's okay," Val said. "I saw this in a boutique window when I went to the grocery store on Tuesday. It was an impulse."

Tuesday, Val thought. Before they'd slept together.

Jamie smiled wanly as she wound up the music box that emerged from the tissue paper. It played "The Christmas Song" in delicate chiming notes. "We don't have any chestnuts."

"Maybe next year," Val said.

Jamie picked up the apple and knife again. "Thank you very much."

"My pleasure." This sucked, Val thought. How do you say what you want to say? "Jamie, I — I just wanted to say that —"

"Morning. Please tell me there's coffee." Sheila made her way groggily into the kitchen. "I need a cuppa joe, real bad."

"Merry Christmas to you, too." Val gave Sheila a sly look. "Up all night?"

"Shut up," Sheila said. "Thanks," she added to Jamie, who handed her a steaming mug. "Can I get another one?"

Jamie looked puzzled, but she poured another cup. Sheila disappeared up the stairs again.

"I don't think she'll be back down for a while."

"I've got this under control, if you have something else you need to be doing." Jamie dropped the peeled apple into a pot of boiling water.

"No," Val said. "I just wanted to say —"

"I need sugar."

Jamie's knife clattered to the floor as she beheld Kathy in the chenille robe that Sheila had just been wearing. She wordlessly handed Kathy the sugar bowl.

"Thanks. Well," Kathy said. "I guess, well, I'm in a better mood today. You can keep your rotten old inn. I think I'm moving to New York."

The silence Kathy left behind was broken only by bubbling apples.

Then Jamie turned her shining eyes on Val. She looked like she'd just gotten her heart's desire. Well, she had. Kathy wasn't going to try to take the inn away.

Those eyes, Val thought. Those eyes and that mouth. That's what got me started. But it's what's

213

behind the eyes that is going to break my heart to leave.

She hadn't really thought about what she'd want from Warnell Communications. She had expected to take whatever they offered. She supposed she should have an agent. But she knew that she would now ask for a filming schedule that let her come home often. And home was here, with those eyes.

If only she could get them to smile at her again.

Kathy left the inn later in the morning. Thankfully, Mark Warnell seemed completely unaware of her presence. Throughout the afternoon Jamie and Val worked side-by-side in the kitchen, staging the preparation of dinner.

Pheasant à la Braise turned out to be pheasant breasts roasted on top of a layer of beef and under slices of bacon. While Jamie arranged the Vegetable Pie and Celery Ragout, Val was in charge of the Forcemeat Balls, a mixture of very lean bacon, chicken livers, lemon peel, bread crumbs, and other seasonings, rolled and then lightly fried in oil. Once the meatballs were draining on paper towels — Val congratulating herself for only having to ask the very silent Jamie's help once — Val turned her attention to helping Jamie with the Syllabub.

They had decided at the last minute to go for broke, and now the Syllabub was just a part of the whole dessert — English Trifle. Val supplied the ingredients in the order Jamie requested, and to her amazement dry white wine, sugar and lemon juice turned into a smooth, sweet liquid. Jamie whipped it into egg whites, then set it in the walk-in refrigerator to set up a little.

Meanwhile, Val soaked ladyfingers — Jamie called them something else — in rum and lined the bottom of what looked to her like a large jello mold. Jamie had already made the custard that she poured on top of the ladyfingers. Val couldn't believe it would all turn out of the pan later.

Jamie never said an unnecessary word, even through dinner, when Mark Warnell could not say enough about the food. He even went out of his way to compliment Jamie on her part in making it. Jamie was polite, but very, very far away.

The rain let up during dinner and Val wasn't surprised when Graham and Len decided to take a walk. Sheila, who had actually eaten very little, excused herself with a meaningful glance at Val and then Mark. Now that she knew the relationship, Val could see the family resemblance — certainly they appeared to have the same instincts for business.

Jamie insisted on doing the dishes, which left Val and Mark sipping coffee at the table.

"All I regret is not having a place for a few rockers so we could relax in style," Val said. "But this is a working restaurant and it wouldn't do to have the customers wanting to eat in a rocking chair."

Mark chuckled. "Well, the chairs are comfortable enough to relax."

There was a silence, then Val said hesitantly, "Mark, I know you said you wanted to discuss business tomorrow . . ."

"But why wait when everything is going so smoothly?"

"I have to admit I'm afraid something will go wrong," Val said. He didn't know the half of it.

"Well, let's talk business. I don't want to get into details, but I have a general plan I'd like to share with you."

"Go ahead."

"When Sheila brought this idea to me, I told her the most important aspect was loyalty. Your loyalty to Warnell Communications."

"I am a loyal person, if I'm happy."

"Makes sense. I'm going to want to ensure your loyalty by contract —"

"Which is fine as long as the contract ensures my happiness."

Mark stretched his legs out, crossing them at the ankles. "I didn't think you'd be a pushover."

"And I didn't think you were Santa Claus."

Mark's laugh was genuine. "At least we understand each other. I can offer you a clear channel to book distribution, cable distribution, you name it. All I want to know is that you'll stay with Warnell. I think Sheila will go out of her way to make you happy."

"I'm sure she'll try," Val said, with a touch of wry humor.

"That's my girl," Mark said. "She can be a little obvious, but there's nothing wrong with her business head."

Val had not been thinking of business transactions, although with Sheila, sex could be a business transaction. Not interested, she thought.

"Believe me, we'll earn enough money to keep you happy. And certainly enough for your cooking lessons."

Val gulped. "Cooking lessons?"

"How are you going to sell cookbooks if you can't cook?"

"I can cook," Val said, not very convincingly. She sighed. "How did you know?"

"Sheila doesn't remember what a great cook her mother was, before she was ill. When we had the time together I was kitchen helper. Sheila can't cook a lick — she'd never figure out who was doing what. It only took me a few minutes to see it. You're going to need those lessons."

"I made the meatballs, almost by myself."

Mark laughed. "Let's not tell Sheila. It would break her heart."

Val opened her mouth to say Sheila knew, then stopped herself. Let them work it out. "If you'd known ahead of time would you have come?"

Mark shook his head. "Not a chance. I wouldn't have believed you could pull it off. It'll be easier with TV."

"Jamie says all I need is practice."

"Jamie is a damned fine cook. I don't believe I've ever had a Christmas meal like that. It was elaborate without being oppressive. I could enjoy eating every bite. Any chance she'll want to continue as your . . . assistant? "

Val thought about it. "I don't think so. This place is a part of her DNA."

"Sounds like Sheila's mom. I couldn't budge her from Cape Cod for more than two weeks at a time."

They sipped their coffee in a companionable silence that surprised Val. "I'm a little stunned by it all," she said, finally.

"I know people," Mark said. "Wouldn't be where I am if I didn't. So do we have an understanding?"

"We do." Val felt a rush of excitement, dread and hysteria.

"And when the lawyers are wrangling and trying to earn their money from both of us, I'm gonna call you to cut through their crap. You do the same. We both want this."

"All lawyers, and plastic surgeons, should be shot."

"Not all of them," Mark said. "But I'd be willing to talk about palimony lawyers."

Val laughed. "Jamie hid some more of those chocolate leaves in the kitchen. Want some?"

"What do you think?"


Jamie waved good-bye to the Warnell Party and the car disappeared into the watery midday fog. If she didn't get this tired making lunch for fifty, why had five been so exhausting?

It had been a vast relief when Val told her that Mark knew who the genius was in the kitchen, but then she'd said that Sheila and Mark were not to know that each other knew. God, it was stupid. This whole thing had been stupid. A colossal waste of time. Nothing good had come of it.

Thank God they were gone, at last.

Val had been glowing since Christmas, when she and Mark Warnell had devoured almost a pound of chocolate leaves and diamonds after dinner. Sheila was sparkling with good humor and even Graham had looked as if his low expectations had been raised. But no one said anything to Jamie about a deal, and Val had spent all her time with Sheila yesterday while Jamie cooked and cooked and cooked.

Talk about being taken for granted. She'd cried herself to sleep last night, beyond Liesel's gentle comforting, and woke up prepared to wallow in self-pity. She'd done well in that department today. Aunt Em would have scolded her plenty.

Val was turning back from the street and Jamie realized that she and Val were alone in the inn for the first time since they'd painted with chocolate.

Surely there was something to do in the kitchen.

She was rinsing out stockpots when Val put her arms around her from behind. She stiffened, then relaxed against her.

"Jamie, we have to talk."

"I know you're leaving."

"Yes," Val admitted. "But it doesn't have to be forever. It's up to you."

Jamie shuddered as the heat of Val's body penetrated to her aching heart. "Stop that. I can't think."

"I don't want you to think."

"I need to think."

"At least take your hands out of the sink."

Jamie dried her hands, then turned to Val. "What do you mean it's up to me?"

"I'll need to live in New York during taping. And sometimes I'll be on a live shoot somewhere."

"And?"

"Well, this all assumes the program takes off, and the book tie-in does well, too."

Jamie wanted to scream at Val to get the point.

"But I'd only be filming five months out of the year. The rest I could spend doing projects, or writing at home."

"Oh."

"Jamie, I want this to be home."

"You want to live here?"

"No, you idiot. I want to live with you. Wherever you are is home."

Jamie had been shocked into silence too many times to count these past weeks. Val did that to her. She stared at Val for almost a full minute, then finally managed, "Calling someone an idiot is a strange way to ask to move in."

"You are an idiot. Why have you been treating me like the plague ever since — you know."

"Because I didn't know how you felt."

Val gave an exasperated snort. "You're the one who ran out when I tried to talk to you. You *are* an idiot."

"You're going to be famous. There are going to be lots of women after you. Sheila was after you."

"I am only caught when I want to be. And you have caught me."

Jamie's lower lip quivered. "I love you, Val. This can't be happening."

"Why ever not?" Val let out a whoop and swept Jamie into her arms. "She loves me!"

Jamie let herself be thoroughly kissed. When Val wanted a breather, Jamie pulled her head down again.

This was madness, she told herself. It would never work out.

"Jamie, oh Jamie," Val breathed into her ear. "I've been so afraid that you didn't even like me. That you thought I was silly and vain and not worth your time."

"I've been pretty much thinking the same."

"How could you not realize that I loved you?" Val tipped Jamie's head up to meet her gaze.

Jamie felt the small part of her she'd been holding back uncoil. Val had actually said it. Before it was too late to pull back, she said, "Because of Jan. And because I know there were probably a lot of Jans."

"You want the truth?"

Jamie nodded and swallowed.

"There have been lots of Jans. But I've never said I love you to anyone. To anyone. Ever. Not in my whole life. Only to you. Because until I met you I didn't know there could be more."

Jamie smiled slightly.

"What's so funny?"

"You sound like a Hallmark card."

"That's the thanks I get for baring my soul?" Val failed at looking irate.

"I'm going to take some convincing," Jamie said. "I'm not the most trusting person."

"Darling, I intend to convince you every minute of every day. How do I start?"

"You start by taking me upstairs."

"In the middle of the day? That's scandalous."

Jamie grinned. "We open for business tomorrow, remember? We're not going to get another chance to behave badly."

\* \* \* \* \*

Being loved. It was a new sensation for Val. Jamie's kisses began gently, then slowly became more impassioned. When Val would have gotten right to serious business Jamie pushed her down and said, "Let me."

Val was panting, writhing almost, by the time Jamie's mouth ended its exploration of Val's breasts, ribs, stomach. She reached for Jamie, tried to slip Jamie's knee between her legs.

Jamie said, "Let me."

She settled down between Val's legs. Val had watched Jamie create the most minutely detailed delicacies and yet she had never really understood the extent of Jamie's patience. The pace of her tongue, slipping through Val's wetness, was slow, so very slow. Hard and fast, Val knew she liked it hard and fast. Jamie was so . . . slow, so gentle.

A fire was building inside her as she surged over and over against Jamie's patient mouth. She gripped Jamie's hands until she wondered they didn't break. She trembled on the brink of ecstasy, but when she finally came she didn't fall over the edge but instead soared to blinding heights.

When she was able to move again, she reached for Jamie.

Jamie said, "Let me." Her fingers slid into Val. "You'll get your turn."

"If I'm still on the planet."

"Believe me, I'm not letting go of you."

Val had watched Jamie flute and pinch too many pie crusts to count. Delicate little motions that required dexterity and patience. Those expert fingers were finding parts of Val she hadn't known could feel pleasure. She thrust herself toward them, needing.

222

Jamie was kneeling now, her mouth nuzzling at Val's breasts. She raised her head, and gasped. "I can't wait any longer. I thought I could." Her fingers dove more deeply into Val and her mouth returned to Val's breast, hungrier this time.

Val met Jamie's thrusts. She knew she was crying. She longed to make love to Jamie like this, but that would mean stopping Jamie, which wasn't humanly possible. Jamie was crooning in her ear, then Val was gathering herself, shuddering. The world dropped out from under her and she slammed to a climax so profound that she saw stars.

As it turned out, the bed frame had slipped off the legs. Val shuddered back to consciousness to find the bed at a sloping angle.

Jamie was smiling. "I have a new project for you."

Val ignored the smile. She pulled Jamie to her, kissed her, then pushed her down into the bed.

## Pumpkin Pie with Pecan Filling

This recipe comes to me from my friend Jamie Onassis, who makes pie crust that is delectable. But we can't all make wonderful pie crust. I will never make a good crust. So I recommend this pie filling because it's so delicious no one will notice you used a store-bought crust.

2/3 cup ground pecans
2 tbsp. softened butter
1-1/3 cups brown sugar
2 eggs plus 1 egg yolk
1 cup canned pumpkin purée
1 tbsp. flour
1/4 tsp. each cloves and cinnamon
1 cup heavy cream

Get your pie crust into a pie tin (follow directions on whatever you decide to use). Heat the oven to 400°. Line the inside of the crust with foil, then put some raw rice on the foil for weight. Bake for 10 minutes. Discard foil and rice.

While the crust is baking, combine the ground pecans, 2/3 cup of brown sugar and the butter and work them into something pasty and sort of smooth. Spread the paste into the hot pie crust you've just taken out of the oven. Put back in oven for another 10 minutes, then take it out to cool. Turn oven down to 325°.

While the crust is baking the second time, get out your mixer and a large bowl and combine the eggs and extra yolk, the pumpkin and flour and 2/3 cup of brown sugar, spices and cream. Mix until creamy and well-blended. Pour into the crust.

Bake the pie for about 45 minutes at 325° until crust is a deep golden color.

If you want to learn how a good crust is made, check out Jamie's new cookbook, "Pie's the Limit."

# Epilogue

*Dear — well, I don't know what to call you.*

*It doesn't seem right to call you by your given name, and I can't really say Mother, either. So I'll just say Dear.*

*I'm writing just to let you know that some things have changed in my life recently. I published a small cookbook and my partner is going national this week with her home improvement show. Until now the show was only seen in major markets, as the TV folks say. But now her syndication has gone national and she's very happy. I'm glad, because it means she can come home for a while. She may even be able to get the studio moved from New York to Los Angeles. That would make me very happy.*

*I'm enclosing a copy of the cookbook. Maybe the sisters can use it. It's easily adaptable to large groups. Wish me success with it, because I'd like to write another.*

*I do think about you from time to time, hoping that you are happy.*
*— Jamie*


I could forgive Jamie Onassis for snatching Val out from under my nose, except that she did it with no game plan. I'm convinced she didn't think through anything — she just won Val's heart without lifting a finger. So the woman can cook. I don't see the attraction.

Valkyrie Valentine is a household name. She's the Martha Stewart for younger women — less fussing, more working with drills. Her *Month of Sundays* book tie-in has her picture on the front, wearing a tool belt and a chef's apron. I know that's why it's selling like hotcakes at stores in the Village.

Valkyrie Valentine was my idea. My baby. My woman. And I ended up with accolades from the Warnell board of directors and more assurance that I'll be their choice of successor when Daddy decides to retire. Not a bad reward. I should be happier than I am. It just seems like I should have gotten more, somehow. I am surprised that I still enjoy finding

Kathy in my bed when I'm in New York. She likes living there. Neither of us is faithful. But I'm sure that Jamie Onassis is faithful, like a trained puppy. I have asked around about Val's love life on the set, but everyone says she's a workaholic.

Nothing turned out the way I had planned.

Val stretched lazily and reached for the soap. Water sloshed from one end of the tub to the other as Jamie shifted position. "Let me do your back now."

"This has been the most humid July on record. You missed some pretty awful weather."

Val glanced out the window at the ocean. It didn't look awful from up here. "It'll be winter all too soon."

"The kitchen is like an oven," Jamie said.

Comprehension dawned. "What are you getting at?"

"I'm not getting at anything."

"Yes, you are."

"You're projecting."

"I am not. You want something."

"I want you." Jamie turned over in the cool water and nuzzled at Val's breast. "I missed you."

"Yeah, right."

"I'm serious."

"Sure."

"It's only—"

"Out with it."

"I just wondered what would be involved in putting in air condition—"

"Nope. I'm not doing it."

"But honey, think of the business we'd pull in with air conditioning."

"I said no."

"Okay."

"Okay?"

"I said okay."

"I don't want to spend my filming break putting in air conditioning."

"Of course you don't." Jamie shifted and then stood up. Water streamed from the body that Val dreamed of every night in her lonely New York apartment.

"Where are you going?"

"Just getting a treat I made earlier."

"You're devious."

"It's to welcome you home. It's not a bribe."

Jamie returned from their bedroom with a single bowl which she handed to Val. It was full of soft, decadently seductive, richly erotic, slightly runny chocolate.

Val inhaled the scent, then scooped up some and offered it to Jamie as she settled into the tub again. Jamie took her time licking Val's finger clean.

Val said weakly, "Air conditioning will take a couple of weeks."

A few of the publications of
**THE NAIAD PRESS, INC.**
P.O. Box 10543    Tallahassee, Florida 32302
Phone (850) 539-5965
Toll-Free Order Number: 1-800-533-1973
Web Site: WWW.NAIADPRESS.COM
*Mail orders welcome. Please include 15% postage.*
*Write or call for our free catalog which also features an*
*incredible selection of lesbian videos.*

MAKING UP FOR LOST TIME by Karin Kallmaker. 240 pp.
Nobody does it better . . .                        ISBN 1-56280-196-1    $11.95

GOLD FEVER by Lyn Denison. 224 pp. By author of *Dream
Lover.*                                             ISBN 1-56280-201-1    11.95

WHEN THE DEAD SPEAK by Therese Szymanski. 224 pp. 2nd
Brett Higgins mystery.                             ISBN 1-56280-198-8    11.95

FOURTH DOWN by Kate Calloway. 240 pp. 4th Cassidy James
mystery.                                           ISBN 1-56280-205-4    11.95

A MOMENT'S INDISCRETION by Peggy J. Herring. 176 pp.
There's a fine line between love and lust . . .    ISBN 1-56280-194-5    11.95

CITY LIGHTS/COUNTRY CANDLES by Penny Hayes. 208 pp.
About the women she has known . . .                ISBN 1-56280-195-3    11.95

POSSESSIONS by Kaye Davis. 240 pp. 2nd Maris Middleton
mystery.                                           ISBN 1-56280-192-9    11.95

A QUESTION OF LOVE by Saxon Bennett. 208 pp. Every
woman is granted one great love.                   ISBN 1-56280-205-4    11.95

RHYTHM TIDE by Frankie J. Jones. 160 pp.   . . . to desire
passionately and be passionately desired.          ISBN 1-56280-189-9    11.95

PENN VALLEY PHOENIX by Janet McClellan. 208 pp. 2nd
Tru North Mystery.                                 ISBN 1-56280-200-3    11.95

BY RESERVATION ONLY by Jackie Calhoun. 240 pp. A
chance for true happiness.                         ISBN 1-56280-191-0    11.95

OLD BLACK MAGIC by Jaye Maiman. 272 pp. 9th Robin
Miller mystery.                                    ISBN 1-56280-175-9    11.95

LEGACY OF LOVE by Marianne K. Martin. 240 pp. Women
will do anything for her . . .                     ISBN 1-56280-184-8    11.95

LETTING GO by Ann O'Leary. 160 pp. Laura, at 39, in love
with 23-year-old Kate.                             ISBN 1-56280-183-X    11.95

LADY BE GOOD edited by Barbara Grier and Christine Cassidy. 288 pp. Erotic stories by Naiad Press authors.   ISBN 1-56280-180-5   14.95

CHAIN LETTER by Claire McNab. 288 pp. 9th Carol Ashton mystery.   ISBN 1-56280-181-3   11.95

NIGHT VISION by Laura Adams. 256 pp. Erotic fantasy romance by "famous" author.   ISBN 1-56280-182-1   11.95

SEA TO SHINING SEA by Lisa Shapiro. 256 pp. Unable to resist the raging passion . . .   ISBN 1-56280-177-5   11.95

THIRD DEGREE by Kate Calloway. 224 pp. 3rd Cassidy James mystery.   ISBN 1-56280-185-6   11.95

WHEN THE DANCING STOPS by Therese Szymanski. 272 pp. 1st Brett Higgins mystery.   ISBN 1-56280-186-4   11.95

PHASES OF THE MOON by Julia Watts. 192 pp. . . . . hungry for everything life has to offer.   ISBN 1-56280-176-7   11.95

BABY IT'S COLD by Jaye Maiman. 256 pp. 5th Robin Miller mystery.   ISBN 1-56280-156-2   10.95

CLASS REUNION by Linda Hill. 176 pp. The girl from her past . . .   ISBN 1-56280-178-3   11.95

DREAM LOVER by Lyn Denison. 224 pp. A soft, sensuous, romantic fantasy.   ISBN 1-56280-173-1   11.95

FORTY LOVE by Diana Simmonds. 288 pp. Joyous, heart-warming romance.   ISBN 1-56280-171-6   11.95

IN THE MOOD by Robbi Sommers. 160 pp. The queen of erotic tension!   ISBN 1-56280-172-4   11.95

SWIMMING CAT COVE by Lauren Douglas. 192 pp. 2nd Allison O'Neil Mystery.   ISBN 1-56280-168-6   11.95

THE LOVING LESBIAN by Claire McNab and Sharon Gedan. 240 pp. Explore the experiences that make lesbian love unique.   ISBN 1-56280-169-4   14.95

COURTED by Celia Cohen. 160 pp. Sparkling romantic encounter.   ISBN 1-56280-166-X   11.95

SEASONS OF THE HEART by Jackie Calhoun. 240 pp. Romance through the years.   ISBN 1-56280-167-8   11.95

K. C. BOMBER by Janet McClellan. 208 pp. 1st Tru North mystery.   ISBN 1-56280-157-0   11.95

LAST RITES by Tracey Richardson. 192 pp. 1st Stevie Houston mystery.   ISBN 1-56280-164-3   11.95

EMBRACE IN MOTION by Karin Kallmaker. 256 pp. A whirlwind love affair.   ISBN 1-56280-165-1   11.95

HOT CHECK by Peggy J. Herring. 192 pp. Will workaholic Alice fall for guitarist Ricky?   ISBN 1-56280-163-5   11.95

YES I SAID YES I WILL by Judith McDaniel. 272 pp. Hot romance by famous author. ISBN 1-56280-138-4   11.95

FORBIDDEN FIRES by Margaret C. Anderson. Edited by Mathilda Hills. 176 pp. Famous author's "unpublished" Lesbian romance. ISBN 1-56280-123-6   21.95

SIDE TRACKS by Teresa Stores. 160 pp. Gender-bending Lesbians on the road. ISBN 1-56280-122-8   10.95

HOODED MURDER by Annette Van Dyke. 176 pp. 1st Jessie Batelle Mystery. ISBN 1-56280-134-1   10.95

WILDWOOD FLOWERS by Julia Watts. 208 pp. Hilarious and heart-warming tale of true love. ISBN 1-56280-127-9   10.95

NEVER SAY NEVER by Linda Hill. 224 pp. Rule #1: Never get involved with . . . ISBN 1-56280-126-0   11.95

THE SEARCH by Melanie McAllester. 240 pp. Exciting top cop Tenny Mendoza case. ISBN 1-56280-150-3   10.95

THE WISH LIST by Saxon Bennett. 192 pp. Romance through the years. ISBN 1-56280-125-2   10.95

FIRST IMPRESSIONS by Kate Calloway. 208 pp. P.I. Cassidy James' first case. ISBN 1-56280-133-3   10.95

OUT OF THE NIGHT by Kris Bruyer. 192 pp. Spine-tingling thriller. ISBN 1-56280-120-1   10.95

NORTHERN BLUE by Tracey Richardson. 224 pp. Police recruits Miki & Miranda — passion in the line of fire. ISBN 1-56280-118-X   10.95

LOVE'S HARVEST by Peggy J. Herring. 176 pp. by the author of *Once More With Feeling.* ISBN 1-56280-117-1   10.95

THE COLOR OF WINTER by Lisa Shapiro. 208 pp. Romantic love beyond your wildest dreams. ISBN 1-56280-116-3   10.95

FAMILY SECRETS by Laura DeHart Young. 208 pp. Enthralling romance and suspense. ISBN 1-56280-119-8   10.95

INLAND PASSAGE by Jane Rule. 288 pp. Tales exploring conventional & unconventional relationships. ISBN 0-930044-56-8   10.95

DOUBLE BLUFF by Claire McNab. 208 pp. 7th Carol Ashton Mystery. ISBN 1-56280-096-5   10.95

These are just a few of the many Naiad Press titles — we are the oldest and largest lesbian/feminist publishing company in the world. We also offer an enormous selection of lesbian video products. Please request a complete catalog. We offer personal service; we encourage and welcome direct mail orders from individuals who have limited access to bookstores carrying our publications.